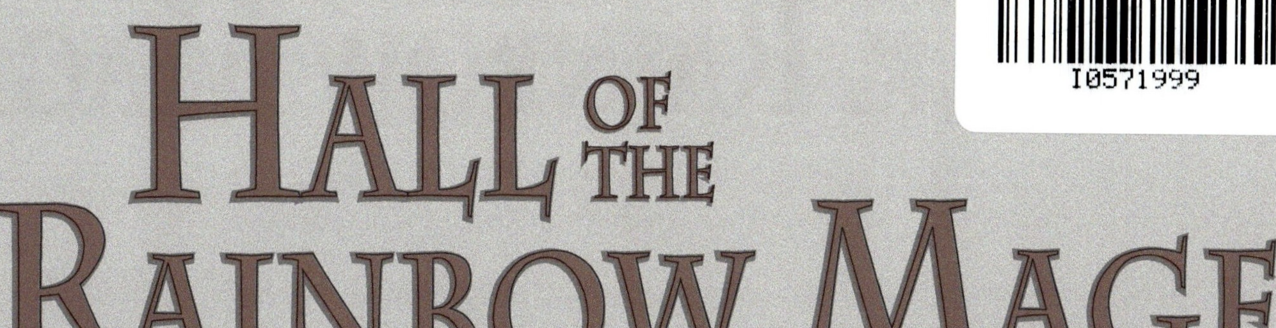

Hall of the Rainbow Mage

Written by:
Patrick Lawinger

5e Conversion:
Ken Spencer with Edwin Nagy

Editors:
W.D.B. Kenower, Jeff Harkness

D20 Content Editor:
Scott Greene

Art Director:
Casey Christofferson

Layout:
Suzy Moseby

Interior Art:
Santa Norvaisaite, Quentin Soubrouillard, Michael Syrigos

Front Cover Art:
Michael Syrigos

Cartography:
Robert Altbaur

Playtesters:
Nathan White, Andy and Amy White, Jenny "Notdatone" Jones, Scott Wall, Brian Shack, David Cane, Beth and Michael Park, and "Gant Burnedtoes."

Special Thanks:
Thanks to Bill Webb, Clark Peterson, and the entire Necromancer Games staff for making both gaming and writing so much fun. Ryan Dancey for creating the D20 license, enabling such wonderful publishers to exist. Melanie for putting up with my addiction and my boys, Anthony and Alexander for helping me see the wonder of the world through children's eyes.

NECROMANCER Games™

NECROMANCER Games
ISBN: 978-1-62283-917-9
5e PoD

Hall of the Rainbow Mage

By Patrick Lawinger

An adventure for 4 to 6 Tier 2 characters.

The following list summarizes the initial actions of the major NPCs in Hampton Hill regarding adventurers. This list is simply a summary for you. Consult **Appendix A: NPCs** for a full description of each NPC's true motivations, information, desires, goals, and future actions, as well as their stat blocks.

Learah Relight: Londar, the Rainbow Mage, was Learah's uncle. Learah is disappointed with the sheriff and the town guards and is actively seeking adventurers willing to help search for her uncle. Learah and her guards have a suite at The Red House, and she can be found at The White Boar Inn every evening. When she hears of adventurers in town, she sends a message to them asking for a meeting at one of those locations.

Baron Kurell: The baron was collaborating with Londar and badly desires some of the items hidden somewhere in the mansion. He plays the role of a "family friend" supporting Learah and her efforts to hire adventurers while already having hired some of his own to search the mansion. The baron also has a suite at The Red House and is often found dining in The White Boar Inn or talking to merchants in the square.

Alfguir K'Eliek: Alfguir is not only a senior member of the thieves' guild, he is the specific thief Londar hired to obtain a number of special items. Londar never paid him for his work, using his reputation and promises of new magic items to obtain "credit." Alfguir wants his money and has decided to turn to hiring adventurers to do his dirty work. Alfguir is staying at The White Boar Inn and is found dining there every day. He is willing to contact and meet the adventurers any place in town, and at any time. He plays the role of a wounded merchant who has lost a huge amount of money and is searching for someone to help him recover at least some of his losses.

Ander Fierk: Ander is a wizard interested in Londar's new discoveries regarding golems. Ander wants the spells he knows Londar created, as well as the methods to create his own army of golems. When Ander discovers the characters are investigating Londar's disappearance, he approaches them and offers great deal of money for the chance to copy some of Londar's spells. He presents himself as a simple wizard in pursuit of knowledge and offers a few potions as a sign of goodwill. Ander has rented a small, private cottage to allow him to watch the characters through scrying and spying to determine whether or not they find Londar's spellbooks and papers.

Mayor Strybyorn Arthand: Strybyorn (male human **noble**) was once a very successful merchant and businessman and is now mayor of Hampton Hill. He can be found at the Village Hall (**Area 2**) or at his home (**Area 10**).

Sheriff Hamra Ranthas: Hamra (female human **veteran**) and her deputies (male and female human **guards**) can be found at the Village Hall (**Area 2**). She and her deputies discovered Londar's overturned carriage and the body of his driver shortly after his disappearance. She is able to tell the characters many details (see her description below).

Contents of Noble and Merchant Houses

If the home of a merchant or noble is entered and searched, roll 1d8 on the following table to determine any contents or treasure:

1d8	Result
1–4	A small, locked jewelry chest (AC 19, 10 hit points, the lock can be picked with thieves' tools and a successful DC 13 Dexterity check) hidden in a dresser (can be found with a successful DC 15 Intelligence [Investigation] check) contains jewelry, gems, and coins worth a total of 1d4 x 100 gp.
5–6	A hidden safe (can be found with a successful DC 17 Intelligence [Investigation]; AC 19, 27 hit points, the lock can be picked with thieves' tools and a successful DC 15 Dexterity check) holds a number of papers as well as gold and gems with a total value of 2d4 x 100 gp.
7	A small chest hidden in the bottom of a drawer (can be found with a successful DC 15 Intelligence [Investigation]; AC 19, 10 hit points, the lock can be picked with thieves' tools and a successful DC 13 Dexterity check) contains a jar of restorative ointment.
8	A thick chest (AC 19, 18 hit points, the lock can be picked with thieves' tools and a DC 13 successful Dexterity check) holds scrolls with 1d4 1st-level wizard spells and coins with a total value of 5d6 x 10 gp.

Adding works of art or other items to different homes can also give them added flavor. Generally, characters should be discouraged from robbing villagers. In addition, local law enforcement will pursue the characters, and the thieves' guild will target them. The guild extorts protection money from the merchants and nobles, and characters violating that protection is bad for business.

Rumors and Information

Londar was very important to the town and his recent disappearance has been big news leading to the creation of many rumors, some of them conflicting. The characters can gather various bits of information either through roleplaying conversations in the local taverns or with the NPCs listed below, or you may decide to use Intelligence (Investigation) checks to determine which rumors the characters come across. Use the following rumors to provide information to the characters:

DC	Information
10	A bunch of rather dangerous looking people have come to town, probably to steal the Rainbow Mage's treasure. (True, several groups of adventurers are interested in Londar's spells and treasures)
10	Londar's niece and her new husband are after his fortune. They killed him to inherit his gold. (False)
10	Londar got so busy with his spells that he blew himself up. (False, but a popular rumor)
14	People have been to the Rainbow Mage's house and taken everything out of it already. (Partly true, looters did make it into some of his rooms and have stolen a number of items)
15	Someone or something attacked and killed Londar and his driver along the Horrik Trade Path. (True, but Londar's corpse has not been located)
15	The Rainbow Mage has been toying with demons, one of his spells went wrong, and he fell into the Abyss. (Partly true, he has contacted and summoned demons but didn't fall into the Abyss)
15	Wizards jealous of his power assassinated the Rainbow Mage. (False)
15	Good luck getting anything Londar left behind. His house is full of traps and golems and things. (Partly true, Londar put deadly traps and creatures in his most important rooms but most of the house is unguarded)
18	Londar ran away from town because he owed the thieves' guild a huge amount of money. (Mostly false, Londar did owe the guild a great deal of money but didn't run away)

Aside from the rumors listed above, the characters can easily learn the location of Londar's mansion as well as directions to the stores and merchants selling any materials they might need to investigate Londar's disappearance. They also hear rumors about "monsters" in the light forest in and around Hampton Hill but a check with any town guard quickly ascertains there have been no attacks in or near the town by creatures of any type for many years.

N
N
N
8
9
N
N
Trade Route
N
2
1
Town Square
6
7
3
5
10
4
N
Horrik Trade Path
N
12
11
N
S
W
E
Map 1: Hampton Hill
1 Square = 20 Feet
Trade Route

General Locations in Hampton Hill

Common Homes and Cottages

Most of the homes and cottages belong to commoners working for the various merchants and craftsmen in town. Hampton Hill is a relatively wealthy village due to the constant influx of vacationing nobles and merchants so even commoners maintain the appearance of their homes. Some commoners work outside the town on farms or in the surrounding forests. Larger cottages often hold several generations, with beds being bunked along the walls and in lofts of the main room. Commoners have very little hidden money and characters should be discouraged from stealing what little they might have. Any homes not specifically marked should be considered commoners' homes.

Noble and Merchant Homes

Hampton Hill is a peaceful, relatively safe part of the world surrounded by beautiful forests and peaceful rivers. Nobles and wealthy merchants maintain vacation homes in Hampton Hill and come to relax, hunt, or simply enjoy the scenery. These houses are almost always occupied in summer and during festivals. Whether occupied or not, there is a 50% chance a hired **guard** is present, and an additional 20% chance that a **mastiff**, or other guard animal, is present. While the local thieves' guild isn't large, many merchants and nobles have chosen to pay "protection money." Theft from these homes makes the characters a target for the local thieves' guild.

While most parties probably refrain from outright theft in town, some characters might decide to search some of these homes. You can create a basic layout with several rooms and use treasure generated on the accompanying table to give the homes more life.

Keyed Locations in Hampton Hill

1. The Town Square

Various merchants sell their wares during daylight hours at booths placed around the square. Fruit and food items are easy to find here, as are ropes, lanterns, weapons, and other equipment valued less than 100 gp. Two town **guards** are always stationed here during the day and other guards and deputies often wander through to talk to the merchants and ensure everything is going well. While evenings are usually quiet here, sometimes traveling carnivals or bards put on shows during the early evening hours.

2. The Village Hall

This broad stone building contains offices for Mayor Stryborn Arthand as well as offices for Sheriff Hamra Ranthas and her deputies. A large courtroom fills the center of the building and small jail cells fill the dungeon below the building. Stryborn does his best to get all his work done in the morning so he can spend his afternoon talking with the merchants and wandering through town. Hamra or one of her deputies can be found here anytime during the day or night. In addition to guards patrolling through town, as least 4 town **guards** patrol the building at all times. The oak doors (AC 15, 18 hit points) leading into the building are virtually always open, even in bad weather.

3. The Hampton Hill Stables

The large, plain barn has 40 individual stalls that run along the sides of the building with a large open area outside the barn to tether additional animals and store wagons. Pegs and hooks in each stall hold saddles, saddle-bags, and other personal items. The large loft above is stocked with hay and oats and other grains are stored in barrels beside the door. While some pay local people to care for their animals, the stables are well stocked and Sasha Blaine (female human **commoner**) has a reputation as a fine caretaker for animals. Sasha employs two addition stable hands, Radik and Danae (human **commoners**) and has enough work to keep all three very busy. Between the constant care Sasha and her hands give the animals, and the regular visits by the local militia, personal items left in the stables are generally considered safe. Horse theft is punished by hanging and is extremely rare.

4. Ebbon's Forge

Ebbon Goldaxe (male dwarf **commoner**) works in this large stone building. One of the few stone buildings in the village, it stands out against the backdrop of the small cottages that surround it. Ebbon lives in a small cottage behind the forge. The building itself has a single room that is dominated by the huge forge in the center. Barrels containing oil, water, and saltwater are lined up beside an anvil that stands in front of the hot fire while bins containing raw ore and coal line the walls. Ebbon is a very elderly dwarf that refuses to make less than masterwork quality weapons and armor because the nobles and merchants coming through town keep business strong. He is happy to repair armor and sharpen weapons but often tries to convince people to simply purchase something new. Ebbon's last apprentice left to become a blacksmith in another town and he hasn't obtained another. Business is so steady that he hasn't kept up on the gossip about Londar's disappearance.

Children are often found sitting on some of the tables near the front of the building watching Ebbon work, and there is a 30% chance someone has come by to make a purchase. Ebbon closes up at night, boarding windows from the inside and locking the massive oak doors (AC 15, 18 hit points, locked and can be picked with thieves' tools and a successful DC 15 Dexterity check) that lead into the building. He stores 2 suits of chainmail, a set of plate, 2 war axes, 2 longswords, a shortsword, and a bastard sword in a heavy oak chest (AC 15, 18 hit points, locked and can be picked with thieves' tools and a successful DC 15 Dexterity check). All of Goldaxe's work is of the highest quality and although not magical, if well cared for will not break or dull even if roughly used.

5. Kyrean's

A portion of her sign came down in a storm years ago, and Kyrean never felt the need to repair it. Everyone knows Kyrean Lane (**bandit captain**) and that she sells a variety of fine goods, but very few people know that she is also the leader of the local thieves' guild. Kyrean sells everything from bolts of silk to fine weapons and leather armor. While she does have a great deal of money, she generally avoids buying anything very expensive from anyone outside a recognized thieves' guild. Although her life as a thief makes her a fence as well, she is smart enough to avoid trying to sell items that were stolen in or near the village. She makes an effort to maintain a stock of rare wines and expensive foods to cater to the tastes of the merchants and nobles that vacation here. Kyrean, a light sleeper, lives in a small room above the store.

A hidden trapdoor behind the counter (found with a DC 18 Intelligence [Investigation] check) leads down to a small cellar where a variety of items are stored. The various items stored in the cellar and in the store above have a total value over 3000 gp but Kyrean's position in the guild makes any theft a very risky proposition.

6. The White Boar Inn

The White Boar Inn is known for its fine food, excellent wine, wonderful music, and clean rooms. The lower floor of the massive, wood-frame building is filled with a large tavern and a fine restaurant. Baeris Blackoak (female half-elf **commoner**) runs the inn with the help of her wife Ivellia (female human commoner) and their 3 daughters, Irena, Karia, and Sindria (female half-elf **commoners**). Baeris has an agreement with the local thieves' guild that provides bouncers and guarantees the safety of her patrons in exchange for regular payments. At least 2 **bandits** are in the tavern during working hours. A human troubadour using the name Khenden Bright Sun performs in the tavern every night.

The restaurant area has subdued lighting and collections of tables and booths that are kept private through the use of carefully positioned curtains. Despite the thick walls, music, laughter, and loud voices echo in from the tavern area, making the restaurant nearly as loud as the tavern. A long walnut bar lines one wall of the tavern with a stage positioned against the wall opposite it. Wood chairs surround heavy walnut tables throughout the room. The tavern closes in the wee hours and opens again before lunch the following day. As a popular place for gossip and discussion, Intelligence (Investigation) checks in the tavern receive advantage. The restaurant serves breakfast, lunch, and dinner, with dinner being the most popular and crowded meal. It is not unusual to wait hours for a table in the restaurant on busy nights.

Rooms are located on the second floor. Each room is cleaned and checked before and after a customer moves into it to ensure proper maintenance. Doors for each room can be barred from the inside, but there are no other locks to protect valuables left in the room. The walls and floors are very thick, cutting down on most of the sounds from the tavern, but rooms near the stairs still get a great deal of noise.

NPC Notes: Learah Relight (see **Appendix A**) and her guards can be found here every evening. When she hears of adventurers in town, she sends a message to them asking for a meeting at one of those locations. **Alfguir K'Eliek** (see **Appendix A**) is staying at the inn as well and can be found dining here every day.

7. Ander's Cottage

Ander Fierk (see **Appendix A**) rented this cottage mere days after Londar's disappearance became known. Though small and poorly cared for, the cottage is close to the Town Square and the other places Ander frequents in search of rumors about Londar. Ander keeps most of his belongings with him but a small chest (found with a successful DC 15 Intelligence [Investigation check] AC 19, 18 hit points, the lock can be picked with thieves' tools and a successful DC 15 Dexterity check) hidden beneath the bed contains 200 gp, 38 sp, and 43 cp. Ander is found here only late at night or early in the morning. He spends his day in the Town Square talking to people and simply listening to rumors, while his evenings are spent at The White Boar Inn.

8. Xanthaque's Home

Xanthaque (female elf **archmage**), an elderly elven sage, lives in this small home (see **Appendix A** for her full description). Xanthaque is a historian who spends her time researching a variety of different things, but mostly focuses on events of long ago. Considered a bit "off" by many of the townspeople, she is rarely visited by ordinary travelers. Books line sagging shelves that cling precariously to walls. Windows are boarded over to make more room for more bookcases. The only furniture in the room consists of an old oak desk, a leather chair, and a sofa with sagging cushions. She sleeps on her sofa, when she sleeps at all, and pays one of her neighbors to deliver food to her. Although her power as a witch is often discussed, few people have seen her cast even the tiniest of spells, so she is rarely beset by young wizards searching for new spells or apprenticeship.

9. The Path of Shrines

A small footpath circles through a collection of shrines that look out over the vast ravine and river west of town. These shrines provide the only location for worship because there is no formal temple in town. Each shrine is essentially a statue standing over a small altar where worshippers may put their offerings. Many gods are represented, and you are encouraged to include deities from your own campaign world. Two additional shrines — clearly much older than the rest — have been chiseled and broken, leaving little more than a base. While Mara Lighthand (female human **acolyte**) worships Arn (see sidebar), she maintains all of the shrines for the gods of good. An elderly priest known only as "Father Rim" (male human **priest**) visits town twice a month to perform services at the shrine to Arn and assists Mara with healing while he is in town.

Mara performs services at the shrine to Arn every morning and performs her caretaking duties immediately afterward. During her morning service, 3d6 villagers, mostly women, are usually in attendance. If the shrines are visited in the afternoon, 1d10 − 1 worshippers might be present performing their own prayers and vigils. While Hampton Hill is a fairly large town, few people in town actively worship the gods, aside from passing worship of Arn. Traveling clerics do come through fairly often, but Mara is the only cleric presently living in Hampton Hill full-time and she considers it her duty to minister to the health of all townspeople as well as any travelers or adventurers.

Arn, Lesser God of the Sun

Alignment: Neutral Good
Domains: light
Symbol: A radiant half circle of bronze, representing the rising sun
Worshippers: Simple townsfolk, farmers

Arn is commonly depicted as a male figure in glowing yellow and white robes carrying a bronze sun-tipped staff. His priests mimic these garments. Arn has a simple, practical, and undemanding theology and is therefore relatively popular among the common people. His followers shroud the symbol of their god at sunset and celebrate the rise of the sun by removal of that shroud in a short ritual with little formal ceremony, uttering only a prayer of thanks to their god. Unlike other clerics, followers of Arn's spells are renewed once the sun is fully risen at the conclusion of the unshrouding ritual. Arn's clerics must actually witness the sunrise and participate in the unshrouding ritual to regain their spells. Some followers of Arn are druids and it is not uncommon for priests of Arn to have a level or more in that class in addition to cleric levels. Such druid priests may be Chaotic Neutral. His priests are bound to heal anyone who presents themselves for such aid following the rising of the sun. Those in greatest need are treated first. It is believed among Arn's followers that the first rays of the sun ("the fingers of Arn") carry healing qualities. Scholars believe that Arn is a debased and simplified version of the greater sun god, Ra, though worshippers of Arn vehemently disagree.

---

10. Strybyorn's Home

Mayor Strybyorn Arthand (male human **noble**) maintains a beautiful, large wood frame home with the help of his servants Miri (female human **commoner**) and Leaf (male half-elf **commoner**). Strybyorn's wife died several years ago and both of his daughters are married and living in distant towns. His servants live in rooms at the back of the home. He is found at home only at night; during the day, he is either wandering the town or in his office in the Village Hall. Walls in his main living room are decorated with rapiers made by different artisans, several worn shields, and tapestries depicting great, glorious battles. The rapiers include 3 rapiers whose ornate designs give them a value of 600 gp but those decorations make them easy to recognize and difficult to fence. He keeps a small chest (found with a DC 13 Intelligence [Investigation] check; AC 19, 18 hit points, the lock can be picked with thieves' tools and a successful DC 13 Dexterity check) in his bedroom that contains jewelry owned by his deceased wife (a diamond pendant worth 1000 gp, a pair of ruby earrings worth 600 gp, and a gold bracelet studded with tiny rubies worth 350 gp).

11. The Red House

Its bright color and prominent location near the center of town easily identify the finest inn in town. Viarik Kite (male human **commoner**) carefully maintains the inn and ensures it is the cleanest in town. Despite the size of the wood frame building, the inn has only 7 rooms, but each room has three bedrooms connecting to a large sitting area. The inn caters specifically to wealthy merchants and nobles visiting Hampton Hill on short vacations. While Viarik usually has one or two suites free, he refuses to lower his prices for fear it might hurt his reputation. Ornate wool rugs lining the oak floors and thick plaster walls cut down on sound, making all the rooms here quiet, peaceful, and very private. The Red House does not serve food, but servants willing to go obtain food from a local restaurant are always available. At any one time, Viarik has at least two people cleaning rooms and responding to customers' needs (male and female human **commoners**) and is always willing to hire more if the need arises.

NPC Notes: Learah Relight and her guards have a suite at The Red House. When she hears of adventurers in town, she sends a message to them asking for a meeting at one of those locations. **Baron Kurell** and his people also have a suite here. Both are discussed more **Appendix A**.

12. Maroof's Elixirs

Maroof Sandwalker (male half-elf **mage**) lives in this small, quaint home, along with all the pottery and glassware he uses to make his products. Maroof is an odd half-elf who has taken a vow of silence. The only words heard from his mouth are those used when he casts spells. He communicates through simple signs and written messages. The small cottage is packed with shabby furniture, and various clay vases and glass vials line the shelves that cling precariously to the walls. A large cauldron stands over a fire in the center of the room. Maroof sells common and uncommon potions for 1000–4000 gp. While the carious clay jars and vials along the shelves at the back of his home clearly contain potions, only he knows what each potion is. Persistent rumors that his poisons are mixed in among the potions have kept away thieves. A small clay box (AC 13, 7 hit points) hidden beneath the fire (found with a DC 15 Intelligence [Investigation] check) holds 500 gp in gold and gems.

13. Additional Shops and Information

Hampton Hill's economy is based mostly on trade, travel, and vacationers, along with minor dependence on grain farming and nearby orchards. It is a convenient stop for trade caravans and a pleasant vacation location. A number of additional smaller stores and merchants not listed here can provide any of the standard goods, services, and weapons.

Chapter Three: Wilderness

<table>
<tr><td colspan="2" align="center">Trade Path Encounters</td></tr>
</table>

Roll 1d20 for every 30 minutes:

1d20	Encounter
1	Medium-size merchant caravan with 3 wagons, 6 **guards**, and 1 merchant (treat as a **noble**).
2–4	Small guard patrol, 4 **guards** and 1 **veteran** on warhorses.
5	Large caravan, 6 wagons, 10 **guards**, 1 **veteran**, and 3 merchants (treat as **nobles**).
6	Heavily armed guard patrol consisting of 4 **guards**, 2 **veterans**, and 1 captain (treat as a **knight**) on warhorses.
7–20	No encounter.

Travel to Londar's Mansion

Londar's mansion is a little way northeast of Hampton Hill and is surrounded by the Horrik Forest, a light forest dotted with rocky ravines and gullies that is relatively easy to travel through. The easiest and safest route to the mansion heads east along the Horrik Trade Path until it reaches the dirt road leading to the mansion. Heavily used by merchant caravans and travelers, the wide cobblestone Horrik Trade Path is constantly patrolled and is generally free of bandits and other dangerous creatures. The dirt road leading to the mansion is wide enough for a single wagon or cart and has no patrols or guards to speak of. Looters who have already been to the mansion avoid the trade path due to its patrols and because there are shorter routes to Hampton Hill through the forest. Horrik Forest is home to creatures and people who avoid the patrols along the trade path as well as the "civilized" realm of Hampton Hill. Most of these creatures do their best to protect their own territories without becoming known by the guards that patrol the trade path and nearby town.

If the characters travel along the trade path, it is likely they meet a merchant caravan or a patrol of guards but nothing particularly hazardous. The dirt road to the mansion is generally safe as well.

The first time the characters are approached by a guard patrol, they are asked their business. The looting of Londar's mansion is appalling to many of the guards, and they do their best to prevent more damage without shirking their other duties. If the characters are investigating Londar's disappearance for Learah Relight or Alfguir K'Eliek, the guards question them briefly and then leave them about their business. Once guards know the characters are on "official business," further encounters with patrols involve waving hands or nodding heads as the patrol rides past. If the characters do not have a clear reason for traveling along the path or if they are in possession of goods taken from the mansion, they are questioned more closely, and eyed with suspicion each time they meet a patrol.

No random encounters occur along the dirt road to Londar's mansion, but you might choose to use a few encounters from the Horrik Forest encounters.

A. The Crash Site

Bent branches and several crushed saplings mark the site where Londar's carriage was discovered. Hamra Ranthas and her deputies removed the carriage, bodies, and any other evidence they found and took it back to Hampton Hill. Wheel depressions in the soft earth off the cobblestone road suggest the wagon was moving very fast when it crashed. With a successful DC 13 Perception check, anyone can notice scorch marks on the stone road approximately 600 feet away. When thieves tried to halt the carriage, Londar set off a spell to scare them away. The flash of fire he created spooked the horses and caused them to run out of control. Once the carriage crashed, the thieves set upon Londar and his driver. The battle was brief but Londar was injured enough to trigger a contingency that *teleported* him back into his private laboratories (see **Map 4, Area 29**).

Searching with a successful DC 15 Intelligence (Investigation) check turns up several empty poison vials and 7 crossbow bolts that Hamra and her deputies missed. While the exact poison left in the vials is impossible to identify, the empty vials are marked with a skull and crossbones that clearly indicate what they once contained. The crossbow bolts are the work of Ebbon Goldaxe, as can be determined by anyone familiar with his work who makes a DC 13 Intelligence check (characters proficient with crossbows of any type can add their proficiency bonus to this check).

<table>
<tr><td colspan="2" align="center">Wilderness Encounters</td></tr>
</table>

Once the party is a mile or more away from the trade path, roll 1d20 for every additional 30 minutes of travel through the forest. Each encounter should be used once, if at all. A roll indicating a previously defeated encounter results in a result of "No encounter."

1d20	Encounter
1–2	A group of 6 **kobolds** attempts to ambush the party but flee when they realize the party's strength. They can be tracked back to their small lair (with a successful DC 11 Wisdom (Survival) check) where an additional 12 **kobolds** reside. They have standard treasure, to be determined by you.
3	**Byorik** comes from behind a group of trees and attempts to speak with the party (see **Area B**).
4–5	The party notices several humanoid figures in dark clothing fleeing farther into the forest.
6	A **griffin** drops from the sky to attack any horses or pack animals the party might have with them. If no such animals are present, the party notices the griffin flying over the forest in a hunting pattern.
7	Ilariak (**guardian naga**) stands in the party's path (see **Area C**).
8	Two **trolls** attempt to ambush the party.
9–20	No encounter.

B. Byorik's Cave

Byorik (see **Appendix B**) lives in a small cave set into the side of a hill surrounded by tall oak trees. Stone benches in the cave circle a small table, and a fire toward the back of the cave heats a large cauldron. While most trolls would have strange, bloody trophies throughout their lairs, Byorik's home is decorated with weavings made of different grasses and branches found throughout the forest. The art, while rough and abstract, is very easy on the eye and makes the cave feel warm and peaceful. Stone shelves hold clay pots containing various herbs and spices that Byorik uses for his potions and cooking. A successful DC 15 Intelligence (Investigation) check turns up a few potions stored on the shelves, including a *potion of animal friendship*, a *potion of healing*, and a *potion of water breathing*.

Description and Personality: Byorik, though a troll, met a druid in his youth, a druid that taught him many things and helped alter his outlook on life. Byorik knows that few creatures could understand or believe his fresh outlook on nature. He stays away from the trade path but the increased traffic through the forest by looters disturbs him greatly. He tries to stay away from people moving through the forest unless they are disturbing the forest or invading his home.

Combat Tactics: Byorik prefers talking to fighting, but when he does fight, he uses all his natural abilities. Byorik casts *barkskin* on himself before openly greeting anyone in the forest. If characters willingly to talk to such a creature, he directs them to Ilariak and to the mansion. He also lets them know that a number of "people" have been going through the forest lately, many of them carrying things. He knows nothing about Londar or what happened to him. If the characters attack Byorik, they find themselves facing a powerful, spell-casting troll with fire resistance. He uses his *entangle* spell to slow down characters and casts *faerie fire* to keep them in view. Overly aggressive or dangerous characters trigger Byorik's chaotic nature and he does his best to kill them all.

Map 2: Wilderness Map
Horrik Forest
North Trade Route
F
E
N
W
E
S
1 Square = 2Miles
Hampton Hill
C
B
A
Londar's Mansion
D
Horrik Trade Path

C. Small Field

A **guardian naga** named Ilariak makes her home in this small grassy field. Now covered with dirt and grass, this area was once home to a small temple. While the temple may be forgotten by most, the area here is still *hallowed* ground (as the spell *hallow* with the extradimensional interference effect) and provides a comfortable home for Ilariak who sleeps out in the open. Ilariak noticed looters passing through the forest and increased her patrols through the forest. She is usually gone during the day.

Description and Personality: Ilariak has blue scales and a humanoid face with a large, flat nose surrounded by sharp quills. Long scars acquired in a battle with a young dragon mar the left side of her body. Ilariak admires Byorik's ability to overcome his trollish heritage but doesn't openly admit it. She attacks evil creatures and punishes evil actions with single-minded ferocity. She does regular patrols through the forest but has increased them lately after noticing looters moving through the forest.

Combat Tactics: Ilariak casts *true seeing* before boldly approaching anyone she notices wandering the forest. She attacks evil creatures as soon as they are identified but is willing to speak with good or neutral characters. She uses *hold person* and enters into melee combat, saving her other spells and abilities for use if the battle goes against her. As a last resort, Ilariak flees to try to recruit Byorik (**Area B**) to assist her if a party is too powerful for her alone.

D. Londar's Mansion

The tip of the tower of Londar's Mansion is visible through the light forest from quite a distance, though the mansion is visible only when the party is several hundred feet from the door. Londar built his modest home and adjoining tower on a low hill somewhat outside town. It is slightly more than half a day's travel by foot and several hours on horseback, so it is easy to scout the home and return to town the same evening. See the following chapters for more details on Londar's Mansion, tower, and the caves beneath.

Wilderness Encounters West of the River

Once the party is a mile or more from the river, roll 1d20 for every additional hour of travel. Each encounter should be used once, if used at all. A roll indicating a previously defeated encounter results in a result of "No encounter."

1d20	Encounter
1–2	The party notices an orcish war party (10 **orcs**) studying them from a distant hill.
3	Three **trolls** attack the party.
4–5	The party notices a dragon circling above a distant hill (not a combat encounter).
6	A **roc** swoops down on the party and attempts to grab a horse, with or without its rider.
7	A **young green dragon** attacks the party.
8	The party notices a cave. As they near it, a **behir** protecting its lair attacks them. You may generate treasure for the behir's lair.
9–10	Two **night hags** ambush the party.
11–12	Two **hill giants** ambush the party in a narrow pass. They can be tracked back to their lair with a successful DC 13 Wisdom (Survival) check. You may generate treasure for the giants' lair.
13–20	No encounter.

Traveling to Arn's Mountain

Later in the adventure, once the characters learn information from exploring Londar's Mansion and their investigation into his death, they need to travel to Arn's Mountain. Though such travel will not occur in the adventure until after the characters visit the areas detailed in the following chapters, the wilderness areas regarding Arn's Mountain are detailed in this chapter for completeness.

The journey to Arn's Mountain is far more arduous and dangerous than the short trip to Londar's Mansion. Once the characters travel over the small river west of Hampton Hill, they find themselves in a rough, wild area consisting of thick forest broken by large rocky hills. Vast armies once fought great battles here, and the release of powerful spells broke open the very ground and left behind scars that still exist today. A rare woodsman might be encountered here.

E. Uvear's Camp

A peaceful **stone giant** outcast from his clan camps here. Uvear has untapped, untrained sorcerous powers that lead to the release of great waves of magical energy when he gets very emotional, even in his dreams. After several disasters, he was asked to leave the clan. He camps here in hopes of coming to terms with his strange powers and odd dreams. Uvear's camp is at the base of Arn's Mountain, and he has investigated several caves leading to the brightly-lit cavern inside. He is afraid to enter the mountain because he isn't entirely sure it isn't simply a vision brought on by his special "madness."

Description and Personality: Uvear is a surprisingly gentle, friendly stone giant. His hairless head and thin features make him appear quite a bit older than he actually is. For a stone giant, Uvear is barely into puberty. He is extremely shy and wary, warning strangers away because he is cursed. More frightened of hurting someone else than of being hurt, he stands a safe distance away from visitors and maintains a stony calm. He forces calmness upon himself in an effort to keep things from bursting into flames or exploding around him. Things have gotten so bad lately that he is afraid of sleeping; nightmares sometimes result in catastrophe. These strange powers and occurrences weigh heavily on his mind, making bad dreams all the more likely when he does sleep. Uvear's loneliness generally overcomes his fear of hurting people. He hasn't spoken to anyone for several weeks, during which his strange powers have begun to torture him.

If the characters speak calmly to Uvear, they stand a good chance of recognizing the changes he is going through (with a successful DC 13 Intelligence [Arcana] check). Once recognized, any character wizard or sorcerer can give Uvear hints on how to grasp and control his powers. Uvear is immensely relieved to discover his powers can be controlled and that the gods didn't curse him. If the characters help Uvear in this manner, he tells them about several caves that lead into a "sun cave" and offers to guard their pack animals for them. He is still afraid to travel with, or stay close to, other people until he has control of his abilities.

Uncontrolled Sorcerous Powers: Uvear has sorcerous powers he does not understand. Presently, his powers manifest in two ways. First, any weapon he holds glows and is treated as a magic weapon and gains a +1 bonus to hit and damage. Second, if under stress, a random object or creature bursts into flames at the start of Uvear's turn (this inflicts 1d6 fire damage to the creature or any creature within 5 feet of the object).

Tactics: Uvear's powers caused enough catastrophes that he was outcast from his own home. If attacked, he simply flees into the mountains as fast as he can; he has no desire for combat or further destruction. If cornered, he fights to clear a path to escape and does so at the first opportunity.

F. Arn's Mountain

This mountain has not been identified as "Arn's Mountain" for generations. Only the books, notes, and knowledge from Xanthaque allow an easy identification of the gray, jagged-tipped mountain as "Arn's Mountain." A great cleft runs down the center of the peak of the mountain. Those who camp on the west side of the mountain first see the sun through the cleft; those who camp on the east side notice that their last view of the sun as it sets is through the cleft. Numerous caves lead into the mountain's hollow interior; it takes a very short amount of scouting to discover several different routes inside. The mountain is detailed further in **Chapter 7: Arn's Mountain**.

One would expect a wizard with Londar's reputation to have a home quite a bit larger, or, at the very least, more colorful than Londar's relatively simple mansion. The house itself has only one floor, though each room has a 20-foot ceiling. The tower at the back of his mansion rises to a peak more than 90 feet above the foundation and can be seen above the trees from over a mile away on a clear day. Londar chose this site for his simple home due to its position above a series of natural caverns.

Walls of the mansion are made of gray granite obtained from a local quarry and are fairly unremarkable. Dwarves consider the stonework solid, but unimaginative and unskilled.

Stained-Glass Windows: All the main rooms on the bottom floor (**Areas 2–8**) had beautiful stained-glass windows that looters broke to provide easy access to the building. Fragments of the stained-glass windows that once colored the gray stone walls remain in many of the window frames, but it appears that almost every window has been broken. Destruction of the windows provides a hint of the looting that has gone on since Londar's disappearance, as well as another sign that something terrible must have happened to him. Only the windows to **Area 9**, which have been magically enchanted, remain unbroken.

Lighting in the Mansion: Balls of glass with *continual flame* spells provide steady illumination throughout all the main rooms (**Areas 2–9**).

Entering the Mansion: The characters can enter the home through the front door or by walking through one of the broken windows.

The Corpse on the Porch: A dark-robed thief attempted to pick the lock on the front door (**Area 1**). The corpse lies in a heap on the low steps before the front door. Decay makes the exact cause of death impossible to determine. Looters going through the mansion also picked clean the unfortunate thief's corpse. A search of the decaying body turns up nothing. A successful DC 11 Intelligence (Investigation or Nature) or Wisdom (Medicine) check determines the corpse is about 6 days old, meaning the thief died several weeks after Londar disappeared.

Map 3: Hall of the Rainbow Mage

1 Square - 5 Feet

1st Level

2nd Level

3rd Level

4th Level

1. The Front Door

The massive front door is made of solid oak boards surrounding an iron core. It has a delicate, well-constructed lock that is magically warded. The front door is the only entrance to the mansion that remains unbroken. The oak door can be unlocked with one of several specifically warded silver keys that Londar created. One of these keys can be obtained from Learah Relight.

Trap: The door inflicts a powerful electrical shock on anyone attempting to open the lock without using the proper key. The trap does not come into play if the characters obtained the key from Learah Relight or enter through a broken window.

Heavy Oak Door: 5 in. thick; (AC15, 27 hit points)

Electric Shock Trap
Magical trap

This magical trap activates when anyone tries to open the door without first disabling the lock, including attempts to pick the lock (the lock can be picked with thieves' tools and a successful DC 15 Dexterity check), but this still sets off the trap. The trap can be spotted with a successful DC 15 Intelligence (Arcana) check and disabled with a successful DC 18 Intelligence (Arcana) check. When the trap is set off, the character who triggered it must succeed at a DC 15 Dexterity saving throw or suffer 23 (5d8) lightning damage (half damage with a successful save). The bolt of electricity then arcs toward the two nearest targets, with anyone wearing a great deal of metal struck over others. These secondary targets must make the same save as above or suffer the 23 (5d8) lightning damage (half damage with a successful save).

2. A Large Entry Hall

Fragments of the windows that once flanked the front door intermingle with pieces of a porcelain vase that someone dropped. The only items remaining in the entry hall, or the coat closet in the southern wall, are large pieces of furniture that couldn't be easily carried away. Blank spots on the walls indicate that even the paintings were stolen. The hallway door to the east has been left open to provide a clear view of the hallway, but the door in the north wall remains closed. The closed door is unlocked and leads into the **Servants Quarters** (**Area 3**). A character noticing the gouges in the wood-paneled inner walls might easily surmise that the looters were in a huge hurry to grab everything they could and leave before being discovered.

Ambush: Note that the three rascals in **Area 3** are most likely observing the characters as they enter this room and may take action against them. See the **Combat Tactics** section of **Area 3**.

Treasure: Searching the area carefully (with a successful Intelligence DC 13 [Investigation] check) turns up a secret panel in the northern wall that slides down to reveal a compartment holding a light crossbow and several bolts. The light crossbow has ornate carvings on the stock along with delicate silver inlays, as well as 18 crossbow bolts.

3. The Servant Quarters

Looters ransacked the small servants' quarters as effectively as the rest of the home. Several cots are turned on their sides, and the mattresses are slashed. Fragments of a broken wood chest cover the room along with small fragments of colored glass. Londar hired live-in servants and guards only when guests were staying with him. Londar placed great value on his privacy and generally had a coach drive the few cooks and food servers he did use back and forth to town.

Three adventurers hired by Baron Kurell hide in this room. Injured in a recent encounter with the wood golem in **Londar's Bedroom** (**Area 7**), they finished resting and healing before hearing the characters stepping on the broken glass on the floor of the **Entry Hall** (**Area 2**). Already prepared to battle the wood golems in the office and bedroom, they instead prepare an ambush when they hear the characters in the other room. If the characters bypass this room, the looters wait until they are in the **Dining Room** (**Area 5**) and ambush them there. The three adventurers are **Violet**, **Kryern**, and **Celadra** (see **Appendix B**, Violet and Kryern are listed together under Violet).

Tactics: Violet, Celadra, and Krybern have been a team for several years and work very well together. Celadra's spells are prepared with battling wood golems in mind so she has memorized more fire-based spells than she normally would. Upon hearing the characters in the other room, Celadra casts *mage armor* on herself. The three move to the corners of the room farthest from the door and wait for the characters to enter the room. Once the door opens, Celadra casts *web* into the entry hall to trap the characters, while Violet and Krybern open fire with their bows. If the characters are stuck in the web, the three soften them up with missile weapons and *magic missiles* from Celadra. If the characters break or burn free, Violet and Krybern stand before the door to give Celadra protection and then the three looters flee through the broken windows.

If the characters don't open the door within several minutes, Violet opens the door and stands aside to allow Celadra to cast *web*, and then the three use the tactics above. If the characters have already moved on, they wait and ambush the characters in the **Dining Room** (**Area 5**) using similar tactics.

Information: Capturing one of the three and coercing him or her to talk potentially provides useful information. Without magic or outright torture, a successful DC Charisma (Deception, Intimidation, or Persuasion) check is required to force one of them to talk. Baron Kurell hired the team to find an ancient text about a pyramid, a small silver and gold pyramid, and a large ruby. The baron paid 5000 gp in advance and agreed to pay another 10,000 gp upon completion of the mission with all other treasures kept by the trio. The information is useful but can't be used against the baron in a court of law because no written agreements or other witnesses exist.

4. The Kitchen

A massive iron stove stands in the center of the room with a large chimney leading up through the roof. Pots and pans are scattered across the floor, along with a variety of cooking utensils. Cabinet doors stand open, and the plates, bowls, and serving dishes that once occupied them have been thrown on the floor. Flour and sugar cover the floor of the small pantry in the west wall. Looters emptied every container and cabinet in search of hidden money. Doors into the hallway to the north and the large dining room to the east remain open, allowing a clear view into those rooms. A successful DC 13 Intelligence (History) check easily recognizes that some of the unbroken china left behind is quite valuable.

Treasure: Although somewhat difficult to transport, the unbroken china and glassware remaining behind are worth 350 gp.

5. The Dining Room

A stench of stale vomit fills the air of the dining room. That, along with the jumble of broken glass from the shattered windows, taints the view of this once-magnificent dining room. Pale wood paneling along the walls contrasts with the dark wood of the massive dining table and chairs in the center of the room. The table and chairs are in complete disarray, and whatever decorative vases or glassware once occupied the table has been stolen or broken. All but one of the small niches for statues and vases lining the walls are empty.

The single remaining statue is an ornate silver depiction of a dragon with its mouth open and ruby eyes flashing in anger as it prepares to breathe fire on its opponents. A master craftsman created the statue years ago for Londar before he worked his own spells on it. Before the other statues and vases were stolen, the silver dragon was the most valuable-looking piece in the dining room. It is really a complex magical trap.

Silver Dragon Trap
Magical trap

If anyone other than Londar touches the statue, it "breathes" a *stinking cloud* that affects everyone in the room. The magic is permanent and can be triggered as often as once per round. The cloud dissipates through the broken windows one minute after the trap is triggered. A *detect magic* spell reveals a complex magical aura surrounding the statue, but the trap cannot be identified by any other means. A successful *wish* spell removes the enchantment, as does a successful *dispel magic* (DC 18). The magical effects must be removed before the statue can be transported and sold.

Treasure: The silver dragon statue is worth 1200 gp due to its exceptional craftsmanship and beauty.

6. The Guest Bedroom

Londar, an intensely private man, has only a single guest bedroom in his home. Designed for his niece Learah, it usually saw use only when she visited. Shattered glass from the single stained-glass window in the northern wall covers the room. All the drawers from the small dresser and desk in the room have been pulled out and overturned, and the blankets and sheets have been taken from the mattress. The mattress itself is slashed and torn apart, and several parts of the bedframe are broken and dismantled. The only item of interest in the room is a small pool of blood along the windowsill. A successful DC 13 Intelligence (Nature) or Wisdom (Medicine or Survival) check determines the blood is less than a day old. A looter rested on the windowsill to dress her wounds after running from the golem's in **Londar's Bedroom** (**Area 7**).

7. Londar's Bedroom

Double doors entering Londar's room were left closed by the last thief who entered and then fled the room. The doors are not locked. Londar created a **wood golem** (see **Appendix B**) to protect him while he was sleeping and to protect his room while he was away. The golem appears to be a simple wooden statue of a tall man holding a large mace in each hand. Londar created the construct with very specific orders: It utters a loud shriek similar to that of an *alarm* spell while it attacks anyone other than Londar who enters the room. Looters attempted to get past the golem, and most met a bloody end. Broken glass is spread across the room along with the splintered furniture. Thieves broke the glass; their bodies broke the furniture as the golem tossed them about the room. Two ripe corpses remain in the room, both in an advanced state of decay.

Combat Tactics: The golem is keyed to Londar and attacks anyone else. It lets out a constant shriek as long as anyone is in the room and fights until destroyed. Fortunately, the golem is keyed to this particular room and does not chase fleeing victims. The golem has enough rudimentary programming to close the doors and stay away from the windows if the characters attempt to use missile weapons against it from outside the room.

Examining the Room: If the golem is defeated or disabled, the characters have an opportunity to search the room. Unfortunately, Londar had a passion for delicate porcelain and crystal, all of which was destroyed during the golem's battles with looters. One of the broken dressers has a drawer with a secret bottom (spotted with a DC 15 Intelligence [Investigation] check) holding several small, unmarked vials (*philter of love*, *potion of giant strength* [hill giant], *potion of growth*, and a *potion of poison*). A search of the two corpses turns up a longsword, two daggers, and coins totaling 14 gp, 32 sp, and 55 cp.

8. The Living Room

Londar used his living room extensively, both for entertaining and for his own reading and relaxation. The curved end of the home marks the base of Londar's tower and has the only unbroken windows in the room. The rest of the room is now a complete wreck. Plush cushions that once lined the many chairs and sofas are slashed and shredded, and small tables throughout the room were broken in vain searches for secret compartments. A wide stairway climbs along the outer edge of the tower to its upper levels, while bloody handprints mark a door in the north wall. Bare spots on the walls indicate where tapestries or paintings once hung. Niches along the inner walls are all empty.

Blood left behind on the door to **Londar's Office (Area 9)** is old enough to be dried and flaking. Learah and the sheriff left the door unlocked after their search for Londar. They were unable to enter the office due to the golems guarding it but determined that he wasn't there.

9. Londar's Office

Londar never allowed his servants into his office nor did he ever do business here. His office is really a gateway down to the caverns beneath his home, a gateway he has kept well-guarded against invasion. The two stained-glass windows in this room are unbroken. Powerful magic rendered the stained-glass windows virtually unbreakable, and **2 wood golems** (see **Appendix B**) guard the room against any unwanted intruders. The room was damaged during a battle with looters, but after they saw what the golem in the bedroom could do, most looters left this room alone.

High niches along the walls hold a variety of delicate crystal vases and statues that are all lit from behind with magical lights. The crystal splits the light into a rainbow of colors that spills across the ceiling in a complex interweaving of color. The effect is a startling, hypnotic reminder of the reasons behind Londar being known as the Rainbow Mage and acts as a magical trap.

Exterior Windows: 1/2 in. thick; (AC 19, 4 hit points each). These stained-glass windows have been magically hardened, making them very difficult to break.

Tactics: The golems stand on each side of the doorway and turn to attack anyone entering through the door while emitting their piercing alarm wail. Neither golem leaves the office to chase intruders. They are programmed to close the door and stay out of sight to avoid missile fire and spells from outside the room.

Note: Damaging area effect spells stand a good chance of destroying items on the shelves and makes the secret door behind the bookcase more difficult to locate (requiring a successful DC 21 Intelligence [Investigation] check) but with the same possible modifiers described below.

Hypnotic Pattern Trap
Magical trap

Staring at the pattern of colors on the ceiling for more than one round forces a DC 13 Wisdom saving throw to avoid gaining the stunned condition. Stunned characters are unable to act or think until the hypnosis is broken by somehow forcing the character to stop looking at the pattern or by destroying the pattern itself. Breaking the hypnosis causes mental pain and anguish, forcing a second DC 13 Wisdom saving throw to avoid suffering disadvantage on all Intelligence based checks until the victim completes a long rest. A DC 15 Intelligence (Arcane) check allows someone to realize the colors could be dangerous and that breaking a single crystal vase or statue should disrupt the pattern and make it safe to look at the ceiling.

Examining the Room: A large ebonwood desk stands in the center of the office, and massive bookcases cover the inner walls. Various papers and books are scattered along the shelves. A successful DC 15 Intelligence (Investigation) check reveals a few arcane scrolls (you should choose 4 level 2–5 spells that the characters do not have in their spellbooks). The desk has several locked drawers that contain interesting items. A bookcase in the northeast corner of the office conceals a doorway (found with a successful DC 18 Intelligence [Investigation] check) that leads to a passage down to the caverns beneath the home. A dwarf or other character studying the construction of the home gains advantage on the Intelligence (Investigation) check to notice the secret door due to the missing space behind the wall in the living room and the wall in the corner of his office.

Crystal light trap
Magical trap

Londar's desk has a powerful trap yet contains only a few items of value. Attempting to open the drawers causes a crystal embedded in the top of the desk to emit a flash of brilliant red light that causes painful burns to anyone nearby. The red light is a powerful, concentrated form of heat that affects anyone within a 5-foot radius of the desk. The light passes above the desk, making it immune to the damage, but any items on top of it must succeed at a saving throw or catch fire.

The crystal light trap can be spotted with a DC 15 Intelligence (Arcana) check and disabled with a DC 18 Intelligence (Arcana) check (dispel DC 20). Anyone inside the room when the trap activates must make a DC 13 Dexterity saving throw or suffer 22 (5d8) fire damage and be blinded for 1d6 minutes (half damage and no blindness on a successful save). The trap recharges in 5 rounds.

Londar kept his most valuable items hidden in his true library and vault within the caverns deep beneath his home. The trap on the desk was simply meant to further deter thieves to allow Londar time to prepare for battle. The desk drawers contain only arcane scrolls (you should choose three spells the party does not have access to) and a pouch containing 100 gp.

Londar's Tower (Areas 10–12)

Londar's Tower rises several floors above the main house. The living room of the home is the first level of the tower. Stairs circle the inner wall of the tower as they climb to the upper levels. A landing marks each level with a door blocking further progress up the stairs or into that particular floor. The three upper levels are devoted to storage or other special uses that Londar considered sage enough to house there. Doors in the tower generally have rather dangerous traps. Londar bypassed these traps — and all the traps in his caverns — using secret command words known only to him or by using *teleport* spells.

10. The Second Level of Londar's Tower

The stairs that lead up from **The Living Room (Area 8)** end before a solid stone door painted in fluorescent red. Soot marks along the walls surrounding the landing hint at a recent fire. The only features of the door are its bright red color and its strange lock. Anyone attempting to pick the lock or force open the door triggers the trap.

Red Stone Door: 9 in. thick; (AC 17, 45 hit points, locked, but can be picked with thieves' tools and a DC 18 Dexterity check).

Fire Jet Trap
Magical trap

The trap pumps out a jet of fire from a magical source. It can be detected with a DC 13 Intelligence (Arcana) check and disabled with a DC 18 Intelligence (Arcana) check (dispel DC 20). Picking the lock or forcing the door triggers the trap. A jet of fire extends 5 feet from the door toward the stairway. Anyone caught in the jet must make a DC 15 Dexterity saving throw or suffer 27 (6d6) fire damage (half damage with a successful save). The trap resets after 1d4 rounds.

Inside the Room: Once the door is opened, an apparently empty room and a stairway that continues upward along the outer edge of the tower is revealed. Londar used this room to store unused furniture and old items he didn't need anymore. The center of the room is enchanted so that any inanimate objects placed there become invisible within 2 rounds. A character walking toward the center of the room bumps into the old furniture and can rapidly figure out what is there by feeling around. The items can be revealed for 1 hour with a *dispel magic* spell or by removing them from the middle of the room. None of the items is of any value to the party. Once reached, this room is relatively easy to guard and therefore a good place to rest.

11. The Third Level of Londar's Tower

Stairs from the second level rise to a small landing before a dull, featureless blue stone door. Anyone attempting to force the door or pick the lock triggers the release of oil from the holes along the floor. The oil pours across the landing and down the steps. The trap is difficult to locate but relatively easy to disable once discovered.

Blue Stone Door: 9 in. thick; (AC 17, 45 hit points, locked, but can be picked with thieves' tools and a DC 18 Dexterity check).

Oil Trap
Mechanical Trap

Picking the lock or forcing the door triggers this trap. Oil sprays out from the trap and affects all in the area. Anyone moving through an area covered by the oil must move at half speed or make a DC 12 Dexterity (Acrobatics) check to avoid falling down (keep in mind that falls down the stairs inflict normal falling damage for every 5 feet fallen). A DC 18 Wisdom (Perception) check locates the trap, and it can be disabled with thieves' tools and a DC 12 Dexterity check. The oil trap has 5 remaining activations before the reservoir runs dry.

Inside the Room: Opening the door reveals a well-appointed reading room decorated with beautiful crystal lamps, broad wool tapestries, and ornate wooden chairs with plush cushions. A beautiful full-sized mirror is molded to the stone of the floor in the center of the room, and the eastern portion of the circular room is decorated with colored stone inlays in the shape of strange runes along the walls and the floor. Stairs along the west wall continue their climb along the outside of the tower to its upper levels.

Londar generally avoided his traps and devices by simply *teleporting* from place to place or by using passwords known only to him. Rune-shaped decorations helped him key in on exact destinations and eliminated any chance of a failed *teleport*. *Detect magic* reveals nothing strange or magical about the symbols themselves but reveals extremely powerful magic surrounding the mirror. The mirror is a *mirror of random portals* (see sidebar) Londar created. When the mirror is activated, it generates a one-way portal to a random location throughout the world. Londar used the mirror to explore the world, always knowing he could *teleport* home when he needed to do so.

Mirror of Random Teleportation

Wondrous item, unique
This odd mirror can generate a one-way portal to random locations throughout the world. The location cannot be determined beforehand and can include any place in the known world, including caverns, dungeons, forests, mountains, etc. The portal never ends up inside rock or underwater but can open to locations with no other exits. Activating the mirror requires a gem of at least 100 gp value to be placed into the depression at the top of the frame. The mirror can be activated only once per day. Each mirror must be created in a particular location; moving a mirror from the spot where it was created prevents its magic from working anymore.

12. The Fourth Level of Londar's Tower

Stairs from the third level of the tower end before a purple stone door that is marked with glowing runes. *Detect magic* reveals alteration and evocation magic on the runes, but the door has no traps and is unlocked.

Purple Stone Door: 9 in. thick; (AC 17, 45 hit points, locked, but can be picked with thieves' tools and a DC 18 Dexterity check).

Inside the Room: A massive crystal ball occupies a circular table in the center of the room, and several strange silver bowls full of water rest on stands in different parts of the chamber. Runes and sigils decorate the north wall above a strange circle of inlayed stone. A small table against the west wall holds a number of carefully drawn maps.

Londar devoted the top of his tower to the creation of a scrying chamber that he used to spy on the important people and lands surrounding his home. He used this chamber to create intricate maps of the surrounding area and to record weaknesses of potential enemies. Carefully studying the map indicates that some of them were created as battle plans. characters studying some of the notes and who succeed at a DC 18 Intelligence check come to the conclusion that Londar was planning to take over the surrounding area by force, a rather shocking revelation considering his reputation as a well-liked, generous man.

Treasure #1: The crystal ball and scrying balls (non-magical) are of the highest quality and would fetch over 3000 gp on the open market. Unfortunately, everything bears Londar's symbol and can't be sold or openly transported locally. The maps and battle plans would be shocking to the local magistrate but are worth money only to Learah Relight who is willing to pay 1000 gp to prevent any public knowledge of Londar's "temporary madness."

Treasure #2: One of the drawers has a carefully hidden secret compartment that can be found with a DC 15 Intelligence (investigation) check. It contains a *+1 dagger* Londar forgot about.

Treasure #3: Beneath some of the maps is a letter written on thin parchment that reads, "L. It appears we are in agreement. The western mountains are yours, may your search of those ruins find success, and everything east and south of the Remick River shall be mine. As we discussed, the pyramid is necessary for success. I shall send a courier with funds sufficient to help acquire the final pieces of the device." While the letter is unsigned, a wax seal has been affixed to the bottom of the parchment. A successful DC 13 Intelligence (History) check determines the seal is very similar to Baron Kurell's, but not similar enough to be certain of its source.

Treasure #4: Mixed in with some of the other maps and papers is a detailed map of the mountains west of the mansion and Hampton Hill. Known to most in the area simply as "the western mountains," Londar's map has an additional message that reads: "Batrie's Fall." A scrawled note near a mountain circled on the map reads: "Arn's? Hollow? Temple?" When combined with other information, the characters can use this map to help locate Arn's Mountain where an ancient temple to Horgrim remains hidden.

THE CAVERNS (AREAS 13–23)

Londar used the caverns below his home as a testing ground and as an extra layer of protection against invasion. Londar used magic and a charmed delver to create rooms hidden off the caverns as well as the tunnels connecting them. Londar installed permanent *teleportation circles* in several parts of the Under Realms and a distant jungle to keep his different caverns populated with creatures to study and experiment on. Some of Londar's research went into creating special forcefields he used to keep creatures in the various caverns apart. Once he finished the intricate network of caverns, he never had to travel through them. Each room he created has a special area with inlayed stone in the form of colored runes that gave Londar the exact coordinates for the use of *teleport* spells. All these areas are unique in design but none of the stonework is magical in nature.

Some of the creatures in the various caverns were deliberately summoned or *teleported* there by Londar; others simply wandered through *teleportation circles* and became trapped. The presence of the outside *teleportation circles* provides an opportunity for you to add new or different creatures the characters have never before encountered. Several caverns include possible random encounter lists, but these lists should be considered optional and used only if you want to create a more difficult adventure.

Forcefields: Forcefields dividing hallways and caverns are equivalent to *wall of force* spells that can be turned on and off with special dials. Londar created a system of dials that could be triggered only by a Small or Medium-size humanoid hand with a full complement of fingers. When turned, these dials open doors or turn off forcefields, and then slowly reset over a period of about 10 rounds (one minute). Once the dial resets, the door it opened closes or the forcefield it disabled goes back up. Forcefields follow all the rules of *wall of force* spells with respect to spells and attacks. The forcefields are difficult to notice without walking into them or hitting them with something, but characters should soon recognize the dials to disable them and that the forcefields are always located at logical junctions.

13. ROUGHHEWN HALLWAY

The stairs drop steadily into the ground in a steep spiral before finally ending at a wide, roughhewn hallway sloping downward to the south. The robed body of a wizard slumps on the floor near a pillar 30 feet down the hallway, which forks 30 feet past the body. The wizard used a *passwall* spell to get through the wall into the hidden passage he realized must be behind it. Unfortunately, he ran into a rather deadly trap. Cautious characters recognize that the body and most of its clothing are horribly burned and that the stone wall near the body shows signs of great heat. A 5-foot strip of floor before the pillar is designed as a trigger for a fire jet trap. Anyone stepping on that area of the floor is engulfed in jets of fire from tiny nozzles in the walls.

Fire Jet Trap
Mechanical trap

Anyone stepping on a 5-ft.-wide strip of floor before the pillar triggers this trap. The trap can be detected with a DC 13 Wisdom (Perception) check. When activated, the trap shoots jets of fire along the length of the corridor from the pillar to the foot of the stairs. Those caught in this spray of fire must make a DC 15 Dexterity saving throw or suffer 27 (5d10) fire damage (half damage on a successful save). The trap can be disabled using thieves' tools and a DC 15 Dexterity check.

Disabling the trap allows the characters to examine the corpse. The powerful flames destroyed almost everything on the burned corpse.

Ten feet beyond the stone pillar is a forcefield (see above) that must be deactivated to travel any farther. Characters studying the pillar closely notice a dial with a depression the size and shape of a humanoid hand. Placing one's hand in the depression and turning the dial brings down the *wall of force*. Turning the dial begins a slow ticking sound as it begins to reset. Once it returns to its original position, the forcefield turns on again. Beyond the forcefield, a similar dial in the wall turns off the forcefield from the opposite side. Londar set up several such walls in different places throughout the cavern's halls to keep creatures safely confined.

14. BEFORE THE JUNGLE CAVERN

A shimmering forcefield blocks the entrance to a massive cavern lit with glowing stalactites and filled with jungle plants. Air on the opposite side of the *wall of force* is far hotter and more humid than the air in the hallway, causing the field to shimmer enough to be somewhat visible. A dial with a depression shaped like a human hand in the southern wall can be used to disable the field for one minute. A second dial on the other side of the field can also be used to deactivate the field.

ADDITIONAL ENCOUNTERS IN THE JUNGLE CAVERN

You may choose to include some of the following random events while in this cavern. Roll 1d20 for every 30 minutes in the cavern, an encounter already used counts as no encounter. The above should be used only once, if at all. You might decide to add more combat-oriented encounters to the jungle as it is a perfect place to add strange creatures teleported in from distant locations.

1d8	Encounter
1–2	A powerful roar reverberates through the trees and off the cavern walls followed by screeches and panicked birdcalls only to close with a distinctly uneasy silence.
3	A **tiger** bursts through the undergrowth and attacks the party.
4–5	A colorful bird charges from the treetops and attempts to chase the party away from its nest.
6	The party enters a small clearing only to notice **2 chuul** at the same time they notice them.
7	Something screeches before running into the undergrowth, leaving behind only rustling leaves.
8–9	A pained wail echoes through the trees, followed by the call of a strange bird.
10–20	No encounter.

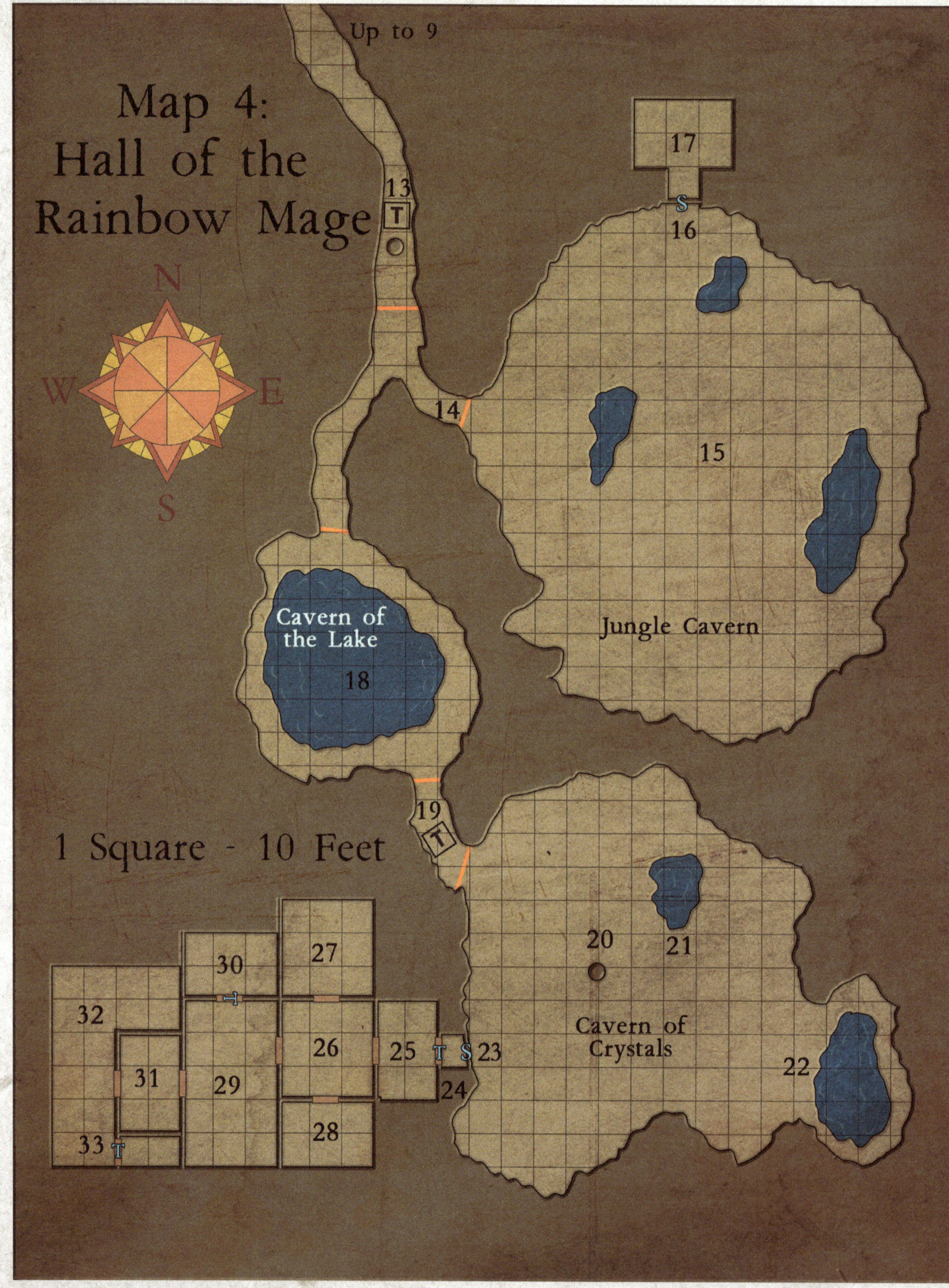

Up to 9
Map 4:
Hall of the
Rainbow Mage
N
W E
S
13
17
16
14
15
Jungle Cavern
Cavern of
the Lake
18
1 Square - 10 Feet
19
20
21
30
27
32
26
25
23
31
29
24
33
28
22
Cavern of
Crystals

The Jungle Cavern

Londar loved the brightly colored creatures he saw while traveling in the jungle and endeavored to create his own jungle in this massive cavern. He used spells to permanently light the cavern from above and then teleported in large plants and a number of animals. While some of the plants don't grow very well, *teleportation circles* placed in several different jungles bring a constant influx of small jungle animals along with a few larger jungle creatures. *Teleportation circle* arrival locations identified on the map indicate regions where creatures might suddenly appear out of thin air. The cavern's ceiling rises approximately 80 feet above the floor with many of the jungle trees planted here reaching the top of the cavern and then bending along the ceiling. Birds, small monkeys, and other animals move through the twisted forest. Numbered locations indicate spots or encounters of particular interest.

15. Kunkthank's Ambush

Kunkthank (**tyrannosaurus rex**, but with Intelligence 12 due to a side effect of the *teleportation circle*) arrived here through one of the *teleportation circles* over a year ago. Although he stands slightly over 18 feet tall, he has found a particularly thick stand of jungle trees and undergrowth where he can hide and wait for food to wander by. While not overly intelligent, he knows exactly how close most prey needs to be before he charges forward and runs it to the ground. Few creatures ever get away from his brutal attacks.

Treasure: Kunkthank has a small cache of treasure hidden in a depression in the cavern floor near his ambush spot. Vines cover the hole, but a successful DC 13 Intelligence (Investigation) check allows a character to notice green stains on the rocky ground where the vines are moved back and forth. His treasure includes some items acquired from two unlucky rogues that came through one of Londar's *teleportation circles*. In the depression is a *handy haversack* (empty), lockpicks, 2 daggers, a rusted longsword, 18 pp, 87 gp, 93 sp, and 72 cp.

16. A Secret Door

The solid rock door sitting in the northern wall has carefully emulated the stone walls of the cavern, making it very difficult to spot (requires a successful DC 18 Intelligence [Investigation] check). Characters who spot the door also notice a dial with a human hand imprint in the rock several feet to the left of the door and automatically realize it must control a door or forcefield similar to those that the characters have already bypassed. Placing a hand in the impression and turning the dial opens the door to reveal a small laboratory.

Heavy Stone Door: 3 ft. thick; (AC 17, 135 hit points).

The door is a piece of the cavern wall carefully cut out to create a well-hidden door. It opens by a series of mechanical and magical mechanisms triggered by the dial in the stone wall beside it. A Small or Medium-sized humanoid hand with a full complement of fingers and a thumb is required to turn the dial; any other hand or appendage simply cannot bypass the magical protection placed upon it. Once turned, the dial slowly resets over a period of one minute after which the door closes again.

A **chuul** set up an ambush (spotted with a DC 15 Wisdom [Perception] check) by a small pond hidden by several thick trees and some heavy bushes. Intelligent enough to realize the dial in the wall controls a locking mechanism, it stands guard watching the dial and the adjoining doorway to learn who is responsible for its recent arrival here. The chuul presumes anyone opening or going through the door is the enemy that trapped it here and attacks. It would attempt to go through the door itself but is unable to turn the dial.

After falling through a *teleportation circle*, this chuul quickly assessed its situation and has made the best of a bad situation. It waits patiently, abandoning its vigil over the secret door only to hunt for a bit of food. Anyone attempting to open the door becomes a target for its anger.

Tactics: The chuul hides in a small pool of water near the door. It bursts from cover and attacks anyone approaching the door or the lock, targeting the person closest to the door as its primary victim.

17. An Abandoned Alchemist's Laboratory

Glass objects, crystal flasks, and strange vases line shelves and benches throughout the room. Abandoned glassware here could fetch a total of 200 gp from an alchemist interested in purchasing it. Shelves along the back wall hold a variety of large bottles made of tinted glass, each with wax-sealed stoppers. A purple dial with a hand impression is beside a set of shelves in the north wall. If turned, this dial does not begin to reset like the dials that open doors or trigger the forcefields in the hallways. This dial needs to be turned for the west door in the **Large Laboratory** (**Area 29**) to be opened. A bench in the center of the room has been cleared of all glassware and holds only a single bottle with a cork stopper. Scrawled words on a piece of paper resting beside it read, "One wish left, don't push him."

Londar actually used this laboratory while experimenting on gorillas and other creatures. He abandoned it several years ago, but beforehand, Londar put a few items here to make life "entertaining" for anyone searching through the lab. Londar discovered a way to transform and imprison creatures in the large glass bottles along the shelves and on the bench. He used this method to store a few of his experiments and a few other creatures he intended to experiment on in the future. Breaking or opening a bottle releases the trapped creature. Creatures released in this manner are stunned until the end of their turn following their release. Most of the creatures trapped in the bottles either attack anyone in the room or do their best to escape when finally released. While there is a **djinni** in a bottle on the bench, it was trapped in the bottle by Londar, can't cast any *wish* spells, and is VERY angry once it is finally released. Characters should be quite reasonably suspicious of both the bottle and the note. If they go ahead and open it, the djinni turns into a whirlwind as soon as it can act and travels through the room, shattering all the glassware and releasing the creatures trapped in the other bottles.

Tactics: After recovering from its initial stunning, the djinni bellows with rage and uses its whirlwind ability to decimate the room. It sends shattered glassware throughout the room and breaks all the bottles on the shelves before using its *plane shift* ability to return to its home. If released in the laboratory, the djinni does not stay around to battle the characters, though it would like to, because it is afraid of somehow being trapped again. Releasing the djinni outside the laboratory results in a full-scale battle from which the djinni flees only if mortally wounded.

The djinni breaks all the jars containing the bottled creatures (see sidebar) if he is released in the laboratory. Total chaos ensues: The pyrohydra basically attacks everything in sight; the troll attacks the characters and tries to use them as a shield against the pyrohydra; and other creatures generally attack anyone next to them. Wise characters flee and let the released creatures destroy each other.

The Bottles

Creatures trapped in the bottles underwent a painful procedure against their will. Some failed enough saving throws that they did not survive, but most of the rest did. Creatures trapped in the bottles are not slaves of the person freeing them; in fact, they are more than likely going to attack as soon as they recover from their ordeal. There are 15 bottles total. If any are opened or destroyed, roll 2d8−1 and consult the following table.

2d8 − 1	Contents
1–2	**Kobold** (any kobolds released are frightened and attempt to run away or negotiate their freedom)
3	**Troll** (attacks the nearest creature)
4	**Ettercap** (if the door is opened, it attempts to flee; if the door is closed, it attacks the nearest creature)
5–7	Dead kobolds
8	**Griffon** (hungry and frightened, it attacks the nearest creature; attempts to calm or communicate with it suffer a −8 circumstance penalty)
9–10	**Bugbear** (attacks nearest creature)
11	**Greater Pyrohydra** (attacks anyone and anything around it, see **Appendix B**)
12	Dead griffon
13	**Shambling mound** (attempts to communicate unless attacked)
14	Dead bugbear
15	**Otyugh** (attacks nearest creature)

18. CAVERN OF THE LAKE

The hallway opens into a large cavern with a small lake in its center. A second hallway exits the cavern along the southern side with both exits from the cavern protected by forcefields operated by standard hand dials. Londar purchased an **aboleth** as an egg and let it grow up here specifically to provide a guardian for his deeper caverns. A narrow flagstone path closely follows the edge of the lake as it makes its way toward the southern exit, easily close enough to allow the aboleth the opportunity for surprise attacks. While it is a good guardian, this massive fish-like amphibian has no allegiance to anyone. It would happily destroy Londar but never got the chance. It knows about the forcefields that trap it here, but its lack of humanoid hands prevents it from inactivating them.

Tactics: Keying the forcefield at either entrance to the cavern sets off an underwater alarm that only the aboleth can hear. This warning allows it to prepare for visitors. After determining which entrance the characters are entering, the aboleth conceals itself in the lake and attempts to communicate with the party without revealing itself. During this conversation, it uses its probing telepathy to find out which party members are the most dangerous and then targets them with its enslave power. During battle, it attempts to use its tentacles to move creatures into the water so they suffer from the aboleth's mucous cloud.

Treasure: Several adventurers unfortunate enough to fall through the *teleportation circles* into Londar's caverns fell victim to the aboleth. It has collected their items into a small cache hidden at the bottom of the lake. Most of the items are decayed or rusted, but there is a 1000 gp ruby, an ivory tube containing 500 gp worth of diamond dust, and lost coins totaling 72 gp, 132 sp, and 259 cp.

19. A SHORT HALLWAY OF POLISHED STONE

A different type of stone, greenish in hue and highly polished, lines the walls, floor, and ceiling of the short hallway connecting the lake cavern with another, larger cavern. The short, curving hallway is flanked by forcefields operated with standard dials. Characters entering the hallway notice that sound is somehow magnified and concentrated by the walls with a successful DC 15 Wisdom (Perception) check.

Sonic Trap
Magical trap

A 10-foot section taking up the center of the curving hallway is really a pressure plate triggering a powerful sonic trap that is concentrated and reinforced by the specially designed walls of the hallway. The trap can be spotted with a successful DC 13 Intelligence (Arcana) check and disabled with a successful DC 15 Intelligence (Arcana). Creatures or objects vulnerable to sonic damage must succeed at a DC 15 Constitution saving throw or suffer 52 (15d6) bludgeoning damage (half damage on a successful save). Exposed glass or crystal objects also suffer 52 (15d6) damage, but objects stored in packs are buffered from the sound. Other creatures must make the same saving throw or gain the deafened condition for one hour. The trap resets itself every round.

THE CAVERN OF CRYSTALS

The massive cavern is filled with strange crystals and bizarre stone structures. Patches of glowing moss cling to the floor and hanging stalactites shed an eerie light that is magnified by the many strange crystal growths throughout the cavern. Londar's latest attempt at creating an army resulted in strange humanoid creatures made of crystal and stone he named "chrystones." Londar used the natural crystal formations and stone of this cavern for his creations and imbued them with an ability to reproduce. Although chrystones have only rudimentary intelligence, they do have strange powers that make them extremely dangerous. While many still follow Londar's orders, others seek freedom. Some chrystones might attempt to communicate, while others simply attack the characters as they have been trained to do. See **Appendix B** for statistics and description of these new creatures.

Sonic traps (see above) placed at the exits flanking this cavern are particularly deadly to the chrystone and were designed specifically to prevent their departure. The cavern itself is very rough, marked by small pools of water and a wide variety of stone stalagmites and stalactites, most of which have crystals of some sort imbedded in them. Creatures living in the cavern include the natural fungi and lizards present before Londar's modifications, the chrystones he created, and creatures arriving from *teleportation circles* placed in various caves and caverns throughout the world.

20. A CRYSTAL COLUMN

Londar's complicated spells gave the chrystones more intelligence and personality than he truly desired. Several of the chrystones used their crystal growth and crystal shape abilities to create a massive column of various-colored crystals that shines with a soft light. The 5-foot-diameter column is perfectly smooth and made from a full spectrum of differently colored crystals. Soft light shining from within the column sheds multicolored light throughout the area. Dwarven characters or characters with stonecunning or stone working abilities instantly recognize the superior craftsmanship that went into the creation of the single column.

The 5 **chrystones** (see **Appendix B**) that created this column are loyal to Londar; they made the rainbow-hued column as a tribute to their creator and master. When they hear the characters approaching, they hide among the surrounding stalagmites and prepare an ambush. These particular chrystones are some of the first created by Londar and are the most loyal to him and his orders. While other chrystones might try to negotiate for their freedom, these attack anyone other than Londar.

Combat Tactics: The chrystones use their *color spray* breath weapon as they close in from all sides and join in melee combat. Creatures that are killed undergo *death shatter* without giving any regard to their fellows. Their immunity to spells and lack of experience fighting tactically makes them fearless. Chrystones do not retreat when heavily injured and chase fleeing characters no matter how badly they themselves are hurt.

ADDITIONAL ENCOUNTERS IN THE CAVE

In addition to specific encounters at the marked locations, you have the option of using all or some of the following random encounters while the characters explore the cavern. You might decide to use other exotic creatures that arrived via Londar's *teleportation circles* in place of these encounters. Roll 1d20 for every 30 minutes the characters explore the cavern. Repeat encounters should be counted as no encounter.

1d20	
1	A low hum moves through the cavern and causes the surrounding rock and crystal to vibrate.
2–3	The party is ambushed by a group of 3 **chrystones** (see **Appendix B**).
4	The party hears the splashing of a **young black dragon** bathing in a nearby pool.
5	Shrill whistles pierce the air and echo off the cavern walls before fading to silence.
6	A **phase spider** attacks the party.
7	A small, harmless lizard leaps from a rock to a party member's pack, and then leaps off and flees into the cavern.
8	A **fungus gargoyle** (see **Appendix B**) attacks as the party walks by.
9–20	No encounter.

21. Slime Pool

A **black pudding** hides beneath the small pool of stagnant water, sliding out only when someone or something comes close enough for it to attack. Its location near a *teleportation circle* arrival spot provides it with a constant source of food. Chrystones living in the cavern are immune to its acid but have learned to stay away from it anyway.

Tactics: The ooze remains concealed in the pool of water and makes no effort to move or attack anything that doesn't approach the water. Enough creatures come to the water for a drink that it has a steady supply of food. Once a creature is within 5 feet, the ooze makes a swift attack and tries to grab and constrict the victim before sliding back into the pool.

22. A Shimmering Pool of Water

Water drips into the pool from the stalactites above, creating gentle ripples that shimmer due to the glowing crystals deep beneath the water. While the glowing crystals might appear attractive to adventurers, they are not very valuable and angering Yorliss is decidedly unhealthy. Yorliss is an elderly female **spirit naga** who made her home here after arriving through a *teleportation circle*. The pool itself is close to a *teleportation circle* arrival point that has provided Yorliss with plenty of food. She and the chrystones are content to leave each other alone because she has no desire for battle and the chrystones know her spells can cause them serious damage.

Yorliss' long, snake-like body is covered with emerald green scales. A series of orange and red spines run along her back and rise up when she is angered or frightened. Her face, though only vaguely human-like, is quite beautiful, and she has a charming personality. Her great age and constant food source have made her larger, stronger, and smarter than the average water naga. She has explored the cavern quite thoroughly and, if the characters communicate with her, she can identify the location of *teleportation circle* arrival points, talk about where most of the chrystones can be found, and mention the location of a door she is unable to open (the door to Londar's laboratory). She knows nothing about Londar and has never communicated on any real level with any of the chrystones, so she doesn't know where they are from or how they came to be in the cavern.

Tactics: If the characters approach the pool peacefully, she breaks the surface a safe distance away and greets the travelers. She hasn't had any intelligent company for a long time and is open to talking to the characters and giving them any of the information mentioned above. If the characters threaten or anger Yorliss, they soon discover she is a canny, dangerous foe. Yorliss remains in the water while casting spells at the characters. She creates as much noise as possible to attract other creatures to the area (50% chance of 3 or more chrystones arriving in 5 rounds). If other creatures arrive, she casts a *web* around the characters and any stalagmites and the stalactites surrounding them to make them sitting targets. Otherwise, she uses *charm person* on the most heavily armored characters and *hold person* against any obvious spellcasters. If the battle begins to go poorly, she casts *dimension door* to escape. She attempts melee combat only against single characters and keeps to the water if the characters stay in a group. If the characters attempt to use missile weapons and spells against her, she swims beneath the water and makes plans to ambush them later. She is very fast and sure in the water and attacks any character foolish enough to try to enter melee combat with her there.

23. The Door to Londar's Laboratory

A well-concealed stone door similar to the one at **Area 16** is given away completely by a marble dial set into the wall beside it. Marked with the standard impression of a humanoid hand, it provides a clear indication that a door is nearby. Furthermore, the dial itself glows with a faint magical aura that makes it easy to see from 30 feet away. Characters within 30 feet of the dial notice it easily and those approaching the dial can make out the faint lines that indicate the presence of a door.

Heavy Stone Door: 3 ft. thick; (AC 17, 135 hit points). This door is identical to the one found in **Area 16** and opens with the marble dial to its right.

While some of the original chrystones are blindly loyal, their offspring are more willful and intelligent. Several have made attempts to communicate to some drow that came through a *teleportation circle*. Although those attempts failed, they still have hopes of negotiating a way out of the cavern. They set up an ambush of sorts near the door to the laboratories. They use their camouflage ability to look like surrounding stalagmites and come forward when the characters approach the door. Although they retain the memories of their parental chrystones, they are more independent and have no loyalty to Londar. They simply want to escape the cavern and have lives of their own.

Tactics: These **chrystones** (see **Appendix B**) do not want to fight and attack only if forced. The leader, a chrystone with deep purple crystal along its arms and head, calls itself "Cliki" as it comes forward with its arms open in a gesture of peace. It attempts to communicate using some of the sounds it heard from the drow it met before, and then using some of the sounds that pass for the language created by its young race. Patient characters may begin to understand that it is looking for a way to leave the cavern. Once communication is established, it offers several diamonds and emeralds — gems it knows other creatures find valuable — for help leaving the cavern.

It is quite possible the characters misinterpret Cliki's overtures or refuse to deal with it. If the characters attack, the chrystones make a fighting retreat using their *color spray* ability if needed. If Cliki is attacked or destroyed, the rest of the chrystones become enraged and attack the characters to the best of their ability.

Londar's Laboratories (Areas 24–33)

All of these rooms were cut from the surrounding stone using magic and the assistance of a charmed delver. The ceilings are 20 feet high and lit with balls of glowing light unless otherwise stated. Any doors in this area not specifically listed as having traps or other locks have the following statistics:

Heavy Stone Door: 3 ft. thick; (AC 17, 135 hit points). Turning the dial in the center of the door opens it. Only a Small or Medium-size humanoid hand with a full complement of fingers can turn the dial.

24. A Short Entry Hall

The door from the rough cavern (**Area 23**) opens to a short entry hall that ends before a 3-foot thick green stone door (AC 17, 135 hit points). A stone dial similar to others throughout the caverns is placed in the exact center of the door. Stone used for the hallway and the door is the same material found in the hallway at **Area 19**, a hint to cautious characters that another trap might be present. Turning the dial on the door opens it, but it also emits a high-pitched squeal that is specifically tuned to the structure of the chrystones and kills any chrystones who end their turn in the hall. Characters in the hallway find the high-pitched squeal painful, but any chrystones that might be with them must flee the area or shatter within one round.

25. A Quiet Sitting Room

Paintings depicting peaceful pastoral scenes line the walls, and small sofas and chairs are grouped around some low tables. The high-quality furniture has been kept clean and polished, almost as if someone has been here actively keeping it clean. Londar set up several different spells to help keep this room clean, for reasons he likely forgot long ago. Once the door in the east wall closes, the room can be considered a safe place to rest. It is devoid of traps and monsters, and there is little chance creatures enter the room through one of the doors.

Opening the door in the east wall triggers the sonic effect in **Area 24** unless it has been disabled (see description in **Area 24**). The door in the west wall is identical to the door in the east, with a hand-shaped depression marking the dial in the center of the door, but it is not trapped.

26. The Room of Symbols

Symbols, runes, and strange shapes created from colored stone have been inlayed into the stone walls and floor. Warm light flows down from the entire ceiling lighting the room as if it were in full daylight. Hand-shaped impressions mark stone dials in the center of the doors in each wall. A careful study of the runes and symbols with a successful DC 15 Intelligence (Arcana) check reveals that most are simply decoration, but some are protective runes and symbols meant to keep summoned creatures from traveling in or through the room. The light flowing down from the ceiling is, in fact, the equivalent of sunlight at high noon with the same effects on undead as normal sunlight. Any attempts to summon creatures into this room or have summoned creatures enter this room meet with complete failure due to the runes and symbols on the walls.

All the doors are identical and open easily with the hand dials in their centers. The doors remain open for one minute before closing automatically.

Londar's decision to raise an army to take over the surrounding area first caused him to dabble in necromancy. His investigation into the necromantic arts was mostly disappointing, requiring more active control than he really wanted. When negotiations with a vampire went poorly, he simply sealed this room with the vampire in it and turned to other experiments. The vampire, though hungry, knows it can't exit without help. Daylight and magic runes in the room beyond effectively trap him here. Unlike other laboratory rooms, this room is cloaked in darkness that extends to the very doorway. Characters without darkvision require a light source to see.

The room is full of coffins, but most of them are open or broken. Three of the coffins are made of heavy stone while the rest are made of wood. The coffins once held minions of Corl Krick, the **vampire** Londar recruited to his cause. All the spawn and vampires in Corl's control were destroyed by the sunlight in the **Room of Symbols (Area 26)** in fruitless attempts to escape.

Corl Krick is an adventurer who deliberately chose to become a vampire when age began to slow him down. Londar recruited Corl, promising him great wealth and a lofty position when they finally conquered a kingdom of their own. Londar helped find victims for Corl to turn into spawn or additional vampires. Unfortunately, the army of undead that Londar envisioned required darkness to operate, and Corl desired more wealth and power than Londar was willing to surrender. A disagreement led Londar to trap Corl and his spawn in this room. Corl went mad. He sent his spawn through the door into the artificial sunlight to find an escape. All attempts failed, leaving him trapped here alone for years.

Tactics: Corl's imprisonment has driven him insane, but it has done nothing to temper his combat ability. When he hears the door open, he assumes mist form and floats up near the ceiling. Keeping to the shadows, he slowly floats along the walls until he is near the doorway. He waits for all the characters to enter the room before floating down behind them and returning to his standard form. Once in standard form, he greets the characters. When the characters turn to face him, he attempts to use his charm ability on anyone wearing holy symbols or the most heavily armored party member. Afterward, he attacks using his bastard sword, reserving his slam attacks for a time when the party is reduced to a manageable size. Any charmed characters are ordered to assist him in the battle. If things begin to go poorly, he uses his spider climb ability to retreat up the walls and to the ceiling where he again attempts to charm additional characters, focusing on characters that clearly cast spells or wear holy symbols.

Treasure

Corl has hidden treasure in the three stone coffins, one of which is his. Holes along the lid and sides allow anyone in *gaseous form* to easily enter or leave the coffins.

Coffin #1: The first coffin contains a *potion of animal friendship* and a *potion of clairvoyance*.

Coffin #2: The second coffin holds several tattered *spell scrolls* (choose five spells that the party lacks, plus *speak with dead*).

Coffin #3: Corl's coffin contains his equipment if he is killed here. In addition, it contains a small bag holding several pearls: 7 white pearls (100 gp each), 3 pink pearls (75 gp each), and 8 freshwater pearls (15 gp each) are mixed with a *pearl of power*. Identifying and separating the magic pearl from the mundane ones requires *detect magic* or other means of magical identification. A *bag of holding* containing 358 gp, 237 sp, and 82 cp rests in the bottom of the coffin along with a greatsword, a longsword, and a heavy crossbow.

28. A Huge Closet

At first glance, this room appears to be nothing more than a massive storage closet holding old broken glassware, furniture, rugs, and a few other items. Several of the items in the back of the room, including an old wooden chest, hint at potential hidden value. Characters exploring the room discover it is really where Londar trapped a **chaos beast** (see **Appendix B**). The creature initially came through one of his *teleportation circles* and created havoc in one of his caverns, so Londar *teleported* it into this room and left it here as a deterrent to anyone lucky enough to get this far into his hidden domain. Designed as a lure to thieves, nothing of value is inside the room.

Tactics: This horrid creature initially hides behind an old chair. It changes in appearance into a clawed monstrosity immediately before it attacks. It waits until a character is within 5 feet before darting out to attack. Runes and symbols in **Area 26** prevent it from leaving the room, so characters who flee are safe from its attacks. If characters stay outside the room and attempt to attack with ranged weapons, the chaos beast reshapes itself to hide behind some solid objects and avoid their attacks.

29. A Large Laboratory

This massive 50-foot-by-30-foot room was Londar's main laboratory. Vials of foul-looking liquids and vases containing dried up herbs and unidentifiable items are stacked on the rows of shelves that cover all the walls. Altar-like tables and long, low benches line the center of the room. Some of the benches are covered with complex arrangements of delicate glassware while others are completely barren. The stone doors in the north and east walls are identical, but the stone door in the west wall is made of a strange purple stone covered with strange runes.

A successful DC 13 Intelligence (Arcana) check recognizes some of the tables as dissection tables and that much of the glassware is designed for specific alchemical purposes. A thorough search of the vials and bottles in the room reveals materials that would be valuable only to an alchemist, along with a few potions that are unidentified (antidotes for the following poisons: assassin's blood, malice, midnight tears (x2), and serpent venom, a *potion of greater healing*, and a *potion of mind reading*).

Trapped Drawer: A trapped laboratory bench drawer holds a spellbook containing a variety of different spells. Opening the drawer without uttering a password sets off a trap that destroys the contents of the drawer and affects those nearby.

Fire Trap
Magical trap

The fire trap can be spotted with a DC 15 Intelligence (Arcana) check and disabled with a DC 18 Intelligence (Arcana) check (dispel DC 20). The trap is triggered when the bench drawer is opened without uttering the password ("Not now"). Any creature within 5 feet of the bench must succeed at a DC 15 Dexterity saving throw or suffer 11 (2d10) fire damage (half damage on a successful save). The trap has only one use.

Spellbook: The laboratory drawer holds a spellbook marked "Utility" that contains the following spells: 1st—*enlarge*, *reduce*; 2nd—*alter self*, *arcane lock*, *blur*, *darkvision*, *daylight*, *levitate*, *mirror image*, *shatter*; 3rd—*dispel magic*, *gaseous form*, *tongues*; 4th—*globe of invulnerability*, *stoneskin*; 5th—*teleport*.

Northern Door: The northern door (AC 17, 135 hit points) opens with a standard dial like other doors throughout the caverns but is trapped. The dial on this door is keyed precisely to Londar's handprint. While any humanoid hand can open it, anyone other than Londar triggers a blast of liquid air that freezes everything within a 10-ft. radius of the door.

Ice Blast Trap
Magical Trap

Anyone but Londar who opens the northern door activates this magical trap. It can be spotted with a successful DC 15 Intelligence (Arcana) check and disabled with a DC 18 Intelligence (Arcana) check (dispel DC 20). When activated, the trap sends a 10-foot cone of icy wind that affects all creatures within its area. All affected creatures must succeed at a DC 15 Dexterity saving throw or suffer 44 (4d10) cold damage (half damage on a successful save). The trap resets itself after every use, but has only five uses before it must be recharged.

Stone Door in the West Wall: The door in the west wall (AC 17, 135 hit points) is not trapped, but cannot be opened unless the purple dial in the **Abandoned Alchemist's Laboratory (Area 17)** has also been turned. Londar enchanted the stone of the door and created two locks as a failsafe in the event one of his laboratory creations somehow attempted to open the door. The characters must break down the door if they did not locate that dial.

30. Teleport Chamber

A decaying corpse rests in the center of an intricate pattern of multicolored tiles set into the floor. These tiles provided Londar with exact *teleport* coordinates. Londar used this as his main teleport chamber for coming to his laboratory and separated it from the rest of his laboratory only for safety reasons. The room wasn't used for anything else and has no other decorations or items. The rotting corpse is, in fact, Londar. He *teleported* here as part of a *contingency* spell and was attempting to make it to his stock of antidotes and potions in the laboratory when the poison finally killed him. His rotting hand is wrapped around an empty, unmarked potion vial. While the secluded nature of the chamber prevented any scavengers or maggots from getting at the body, bacteria have already begun their slow decay of the corpse. Characters might wish to somehow *speak with dead* or use other spells to communicate with Londar. For the purpose of spells, Londar has been dead for four weeks plus the number of days it has taken characters to get this far. Londar generally answers poorly worded questions with riddles or questions, but carefully worded questions provide useful information (see Londar's Information sidebox). Londar felt safe and really wasn't carrying much with him when he left for his niece's wedding, so his corpse carries less treasure than the characters might hope.

Treasure: Londar's corpse wears a signet ring (20 gp) that should make it clear that this is his corpse. They can also find the following items: a brightly colored cloak, a *ring of protection*, a *wand of fireballs*, a money bag holding 58 gp, 73 sp, and 2 cp, and a spellbook containing the following spells: 1st—*alarm, charm person, color spray, mage armor, shield*; 2nd—*arcane lock, invisibility, see invisibility, web*; 3rd—*dispel magic, fireball, haste, major image*; 4th—*dimension door, rainbow spear*, wall of fire*; 5th—*contact other plane, geas, rainbow staff*, teleportation circle*; 6th—*contingency, programmed illusion, sunbeam*; 7th—*magnificent mansion, prismatic spray, teleport*; 8th—*control weather, dominate monster, mind blank*; 9th—*gate, teleport other*, prismatic wall, time stop*.

* Spell created by Londar that appears in **Appendix E**.

Londar's Information

If the characters use a *speak with dead* spell (a scroll with this spell is found in **Area 27**) to question Londar, they can learn some useful facts. A few sample questions and answers are listed below. Adjudicate other questions, as Londar's corpse avoids giving information about what *Horgrim's Pyramid* does, specifically naming Baron Kurell, or telling the characters how to open his vault.

Question	Response
Who killed you?	Thieves, who else? Lucky bastards, too. Poisoned me.
Why were you killed?	I suppose the baron didn't pay my bills as he promised. Probably wants the pyramid for himself.
What bills?	The bills the baron was supposed to pay.
Which baron?	The one that was supposed to pay the thieves' guild.
What pyramid?	*Horgrim's Pyramid.*
What does the pyramid do?	Enough to kill for.
Why do you owe the thieves' guild money?	We hired Alfguir to steal a few things for us.
How do you open the vault?	I generally just turn the dial with my hand.
Is the vault trapped?	Certainly.

31. The Summoning Chamber

This summoning chamber is heavily warded and protected. Summoned creatures cannot even touch the doors, let alone escape. Powerful runes and symbols adorn the walls and ceiling and prevent summoning anywhere other than the center of the circle of runes in the middle of the room. These same runes prevent any form of ethereal travel or *gate* or *teleport* spells. Londar used this chamber to summon and talk to demons and other powerful creatures and depended on his protective spells to keep the summoned creatures trapped here until he released them.

Londar's most recent discussion was with a demon named Iriala (**succubus/incubus**) who remains trapped in the room since the mage's death. Iriala desperately wants to escape the room but knows the only way out is to be invited by someone unaffected by the imprisoning spells. Londar normally entered through the western door from the library, and his long absence bothers Iriala, who fears being forgotten by the mage or of something happening to Londar. Upon hearing the click of the door mechanism, Iriala prepares to meet anyone coming through as described below.

Tactics: Iriala has been trapped for more than a month. The magic of the room prevents them from using their etherealness. They must be invited out of the room by another free-willed being (charmed characters or NPCs do not count). Once free of this room, they can use all their abilities.

Iriala's primary goal is to obtain their freedom. When the door from the laboratory, a door Londar never used, opens, they use their shapechange ability to take the shape of a handsome male human wearing expensive clothing. Using that form, Iriala greets the characters joyfully and thanks them for rescuing him. Claiming to be a kidnapped victim, Iriala begs the characters to escort him out of "Londar's horrible dungeon." Iriala uses different tactics against the characters depending upon whether or not they invite them to travel with them, thereby releasing them, or see through their ruse and refuse to help them.

If the characters invite them along, they continue in their male human form, with the goal of letting the characters obtain treasure for them before they flee. They surreptitiously attempt to charm any character that shows interest, but take advantage of their draining kiss only in privacy. Otherwise, they wait for a good moment to loot the characters before fleeing through the Ethereal Plane. They use any charmed characters to foster confusion and use their draining kiss ability on any character they attack. If the battle goes against them, Iriala flees to the Ethereal Plane, stealing as many items as possible.

The characters are likely to find Iriala's male form and story of kidnapping different enough to be believable, but they might also notice that the doors out of the room open easily and might wonder why he didn't try to leave on his own. If the characters see through their ruse and refuse to release them, Iriala flees.

Londar's library is, in a word, magnificent. Londar *teleported* highly paid craftsmen into the room along with the wood and materials they needed to do their work. Dark brown leather chairs surround mahogany tables in the center of the room, and mahogany bookcases with intricate carvings line the walls all the way up to the high ceiling. Rolling ladders attached to the bookshelves allow access to books on the highest shelves. A diffuse light comes down from the ceiling, lighting the room evenly for reading and studying. Beautiful wool rugs cover the stone floors in all but the northeast corner, which is coated with colored tiles in the shape of intricate runes. The only doors in the room include the stone door leading back into the **Summoning Chamber (Area 31)** and the heavy steel door into **Londar's Vault (Area 33)** located at the southernmost end of the east wall.

Books lining the shelves cover a wide variety of subjects and include works of poetry and fiction along with texts on warfare, military organization, construction, and other rather dry subjects. Londar knew where he put different books and never took the time to organize his library beyond keeping books he used most often on the lower shelves. Books containing magic spells are mixed together with the other texts and take some searching to identify.

The library is protected by 3 **wood golems** (AC 15 due to the quality of their wooden bodies, see **Appendix B**) keyed specifically to Londar. These golems are similar to those in **Area 7** but are made from the same mahogany as the rest of the furniture in the library and are carved in the form of robed humans with clenched fists.

Tactics: The golems rush forward, screeching their alarm, and attack anyone other than Londar. They close for melee combat with their chosen target(s) and fight until destroyed. These golems follow fleeing characters as far as the **Laboratory (Area 29)** but go no farther. Doors that close automatically and prevent their return to the library might effectively trap them in a different room.

Battle with the wood golems stands a chance of damaging books and other items in the library. Carefully monitor the use of any area spells or fire-based spells and inflict damage on items within the library as needed.

Treasure: Finding the various spellbooks requires some time searching, so each spellbook is given a different DC. Characters searching with the assistance of a *detect magic* spell receive advantage on their search for spellbooks.

Spellbook #1: DC 11 Intelligence (Investigation) check; contains the following spells: 0—all; 1st—all. This book is trapped with the *glyph of warding* spell (explosive runes) triggered by anyone reading the first page. It is a DC 18 to save against the spell.

Spellbook #2: DC 13 Intelligence (Investigation) check; contains the following spells: 4th—*banishment*; 5th—*passwall*; 7th—*force cage, prismatic spray*; 9th—*prismatic wall*. This book is trapped with the *glyph of warding* spell (spell glyph: *confusion*) triggered by anyone reading the 50th page. It is a DC 18 to save against the spell.

Spellbook #3: DC 18 Intelligence (Investigation) check; contains the following spells: 7th—*prismatic spray, sequester, teleport*; 8th—*antimagic field, demiplane*; 9th—*teleport other**.

Spellbook #4: DC 18 Intelligence (Investigation) check; contains the following spells: 2nd—*blur, continual flame, detect thoughts, flaming sphere, mirror image, rope trick*; 3rd—*fireball, fly, glyph of warding, hold person, tiny hut, lightning bolt*; 4th—*dimensional door, fire shield, rainbow spear**. This book is trapped with *explosive runes* exactly the same way as spellbook #1.

Spellbook #5: DC 18 Intelligence (Investigation) check; 4th—*arcane eye, banishment, greater invisibility, fabricate, ice storm, locate creature, rainbow spear**; 5th—*contact other plane, dominate person, geas, rainbow staff**.

* Spell created by Londar that appears in **Appendix E**.

Treasure: In addition to the spellbooks, several other interesting texts are stored in the library. Each requires a DC 18 Intelligence (Investigation) check to find:

- Two matched books known as the *Arcanari**
- *Jaerel's Jungle Guide**
- Several ancient texts describing the process to magically harden and reinforce stone (worth 2000 gp)
- Book describing how to create wood golems found throughout Londar's home (worth 1000 gp)
- Book describing several foul uses for dragon blood (worth 300 gp)

* See **Appendix D: New Magic Items**
The ornate wool rugs are heavy and difficult to move but have a total value of 2700 gp.

The massive steel vault is covered with strange, glowing runes and sigils that surround yet another handprint lock. While any small or medium-size hand can unlock the vault, only Londar's hand can open the vault without setting off a very deadly *chain lightning trap*.

Steel Vault Door: 15 in. thick; (AC 19, 55 hit points). The enchanted steel door is counterweighted to open and close easily once unlocked.

Chain Lightning Trap
Magical Trap

This trap triggers when someone other than Londar opens the door to his vault. The trap can be spotted with a DC 18 Intelligence (Arcana) check and disabled with a DC 22 Intelligence (Arcana) check (dispel DC 22). Once triggered, the trap fires a lightning bolt at the creature nearest the door. This bolt then branches off to hit up to 10 characters within 30 feet of the door. The trap makes an attack roll with a +15 modifier; targets wearing metal armor or carrying a large amount of metal are attacked with advantage. The first bolt inflicts 45 (10d8) lightning damage; secondary bolts inflict 27 (6d8) lightning damage.

Note: If the characters haven't learned caution after the door to the **Teleport Chamber (Area 30)**, this trap has the potential to kill many in the party.

In addition to spellbooks containing all or some of the spells found in **Areas 29, 30,** and **32** (your choice), the characters find a book describing a process to colorize spells and a variety of papers and documents describing Londar's experiments. When combined with the maps and battle plans found in the **Fourth Level of Londar's Tower (Area 12)**, the papers and documents the characters find here provide undeniable proof that Londar was planning to brutally conquer the surrounding area with the help of an unidentified baron.

Treasure: *Rainbow bracers*, rainbow ring*, rainbow crossbow*, Horgrim Pyramid*, Korik's Ruby**, the *Decaying Book**, and gold and gems with a total value of 45,000 gp.

* See **Appendix D**

After learning what happened to Londar, the party is almost certain to return to Hampton Hill with their newfound knowledge, treasure, and possibly Londar's corpse.

Ambush!

Unfortunately, **Ander Fierk** (see **Appendix A**) has been scrying on the party to determine whether or not they have been successful. Once he learns they have some of Londar's spellbooks and papers, he decides to ambush the party along the road back to Hampton Hill.

Tactics: Ander, in his quest for power and knowledge, has joined forces with Baron Kurell. His mission is to obtain Londar's spellbooks, notes, and any evidence mentioning the baron. He casts *alter self* to alter his appearance to avoid being identified in the event he fails or someone gets away. He then casts *fly*. Once prepared, he flies above the path or road the characters are using and waits for them to approach his position. He attempts to capture the characters with a *black tentacles* spell. If the battle goes against him, Ander is a coward; he uses his *fly* spell to remain high above the characters and rains fireballs down on them. He retreats if he takes more than 20 points of damage and leaves the area to meet with Baron Kurell (see below).

Note: Ander's preparations give him a distinct advantage. If the characters succeed in bringing him down, a 10% experience bonus is suggested.

Arriving in Hampton Hill

After the ambush, the characters are likely injured, tired, angry, and somewhat suspicious. Finally reaching Hampton Hill doesn't turn out to be very relaxing.

Their return is met with joy and sorrow as other things have happened in their absence. After their return, Sheriff Hamra Ranthas summons the characters. Hamra and the mayor inform the characters that Baron Kurell and his men tortured and left for dead Xanthaque, an elderly elven witch living in town. Xanthaque did not reveal what they were searching for but did tell the sheriff that she gave them wrong directions. The sheriff tells the characters that pigeons have gone out with information about the baron's destination and that the king has sent guards to arrest him. Based on comments Xanthaque made, Hamra is concerned about potential threats to the town. She asks the characters to speak to Xanthaque and ensure there are no other threats to Hampton Hill.

Returning Londar's corpse and the incriminating papers to Learah Relight should garner a reasonable monetary reward and a small experience point reward. Upon the return of her uncle's corpse, Learah makes immediate plans to have him *resurrected*. Learah also most likely claims her father's spellbooks as her property by right, though she allows character spellcasters to copy spells from them. She also may (at your discretion) claim any of the major magic items recovered from the mansion as hers by inheritance.

Attempts to contact Ander Fierk (presuming he escaped the ambush without being identified) end in failure. Questions regarding Ander's whereabouts cause several people to say that he left with Baron Kurell, a rumor Learah and Xanthaque can confirm (see below).

If the characters follow up on the sheriff's request and visit Xanthaque (female elf **archmage**), she weaves a tale that sends them off on another, possibly more dangerous, journey.

Despite the healing and ministering she has received, Xanthaque's age makes recovery from her ordeal rather lengthy. Xanthaque informs the characters that Baron Kurell is really a cleric worshipping Orcus and that he somehow found out about an artifact known as *The White Eye*. While she doesn't know the exact details about the eye, she knows it is an extremely powerful, evil relic. Xanthaque provides the characters with sketchy information about a forgotten evil god known as "Horgrim" and the great battles between his forces and forces worshipping Arn (see the information previously provided regarding Arn's Mountain).

If the characters provide her with the *Decaying Book* (**Area 33** of the **Mansion**), maps, and other documents found in **Areas 12** and **33**, she interprets the book and tell the characters the properties of the activated pyramid. If the characters let her, she dispels some of the spells on the pyramid and asks them to melt it down. Although she is unable to identify the exact powers the eye is supposed to possess, she is certain that it is extremely powerful and should never find its way into the wrong hands. She tells the characters that she sent Baron Kurell in the wrong direction but believes he will escape capture and eventually discover the eye's location.

The maps and notes discovered in Londar's mansion and library allow her to provide the characters with a location for "Arn's Mountain," a hollow mountain reported to hold an ancient temple to Horgrim, the last known refuge for Horgrim's followers and *The White Eye*. If the characters seem hesitant, Xanthaque describes the vast wealth Horgrim's followers reportedly hid deep inside their temples and even goes as far as to offer a few magic items. After her torture, she is desperate to foil any plans the baron might have and is honestly afraid of the powers the eye might possess.

CONTINUING THE ADVENTURE

Learah recovers her beloved uncle's corpse and travels to a major city to have him *resurrected*. Londar's paranoia leads him to *teleport* to a distant jungle hideaway and begin making new plans. While he might eventually plot against the characters, he has more pressing plans to make regarding Alfguir and the baron and is desperately short of funds. If the characters introduce some of the items they found as evidence against Baron Kurell and Londar, they find that their information simply isn't important when compared to Xanthaque's testimony about the baron's torture.

The characters might decide to act on information suggesting Alfguir is somehow responsible for Londar's death or that he is a member of the thieves' guild. If they question Alfguir, they find themselves up against an intelligent, wily thief who has learned many tricks for fooling spells aimed at determining truth (see below).

QUESTIONING ALFGUIR

Alfguir is a successful merchant and a successful thief due to his intelligence. He does an excellent job of avoiding accusations and redirecting accusations made against him. If the characters do question Alfguir, he avoids telling direct lies, but also avoids revealing much of the truth. One point that should be remembered is that Alfguir suspects his people killed Londar but doesn't know for certain, and he did not order them to do so. Londar's death disappoints him because all he really wanted was payment. This means that he can honestly say he did not know about or order Londar's death. If asked if he is a thief, Alfguir replies, "Well, someone always claims a merchant has robbed them, so I suppose you can find someone that will say I am." If asked if he is a member of the thieves' guild, Alfguir replies, "I am a member of many guilds, some admittedly with bad reputations, but all traveling merchants must make these sacrifices."

In general, the characters do not have enough information to accuse Alfguir of breaking any laws, and he avoids giving them any. Alfguir makes certain to depart for distant cities if he discovers the characters have any inkling of his true business. If the characters are clever enough about their questioning and avoid making any accusations, Alfguir might reveal he was hired to "acquire" a few rather strange items pictured in a book and used his contacts to eventually purchase them for Londar (Gather Information check DC 20).

CHAPTER SEVEN: ARN'S MOUNTAIN

BACKGROUND

Horgrim's followers once captured vast territories, but their success also led to their downfall. Using the many relics and artifacts they possessed depended upon cooperation, teamwork, and a strict adherence to hierarchy. Political ambitions and infighting broke down the hierarchy, leading many different factions to break apart, with each taking different relics and pieces of relics with them. Forces worshipping the good gods were quick to take advantage of their lack of order. Successive battles broke down and destroyed many of the different factions until one main faction remained. A last effort was made to create a hidden temple within the recesses of a hollow mountain. Designed as a place to gather Horgrim's remaining forces and artifacts and eventually rebuild the great armies they once possessed, it became a focal point not just for Horgrim's followers, but also for followers of the good gods, particularly Arn, one of Horgrim's main opponents.

Several rangers dedicated to Arn discovered the hollow mountain and instigated an all-out attack against the temple hidden within it. After terrible losses, Arn's forces took the cavern and trapped all of Horgrim's followers inside their temple. All efforts to invade the temple itself were repelled, sometimes by traps, other times by soldiers or magic. Arn's forces had few remaining leaders after these battles, but all of them reached the same conclusion: The cost of taking the temple was too high. It would be easier to keep the denizens of the temple trapped inside until they died of starvation, thirst, or old age.

The rock of the high ceiling was imbued with magical sunlight using complex rituals, and magical creatures were asked to guard the temple and prevent Horgrim's trapped followers from ever departing. With the outside of the temple securely guarded, the priests and faithful servants to Horgrim inside used their time to create numerous deadly traps to help protect their relics from Arn's forces. Some of the followers chose death, while others willing turned to a life of undead servitude in Horgrim's name. A few chosen followers were frozen in time, awaiting a day when they could again form armies in Horgrim's name and march forth on the world.

Over the centuries, some guardians left for other duties or died without passing the duty to another. A few magical creatures remain, guarding the temple as a duty handed down through generations with no real knowledge of why. Years of constant sunlight and moisture, along with seeds brought in by passing birds and animals, helped the cavern develop lush, rich vegetation that supports a variety of wildlife.

ARN'S MOUNTAIN

Bright, magical sunlight constantly flows from the high ceiling of the hollowed-out mountain to feed the many plants and mosses that grow in the moist, warm air. A number of animals make their winter, or even permanent, homes here, with some of them growing far larger than normal. The high ceiling varies from 600 to 800 feet above the rolling floor and the hollowed-out mountain itself has a radius of roughly 2000 feet. A strange, tiered temple stands in the southwest corner, oddly free of the many vines and mosses that cover almost every other surface. While there are numerous exits and entrances to the hollow chamber, most are quite small, and all are at least 100 feet above the ground, forcing creatures entering or leaving to either climb the walls or fly. Numerous pools of water dot the cavern, along with clusters of large trees grown from seeds carried by birds or other animals.

The most dangerous creatures in the cavern are undoubtedly the **couatl** that stand watch over the temple. Other creatures in the cavern are generally frightened enough of armed humanoids to stay far away. The only creature that might cause trouble is the tiger lord that doesn't like anyone interfering with its territory (see **Area A**).

Horgrim, God of War and Magic

Alignment: Lawful Evil
Domains: war, undeath
Symbol: A black spearhead covering a gold disc that represents an eclipse.
Worshippers: Evil monks, warriors, wizards, and nobles.
Favored Weapons: Shortspear, staff

Horgrim is commonly depicted as a handsome male figure in black robes wielding a shortspear. Almost forgotten now, Horgrim was a popular god several millennia ago but political fighting among his priests led to a rapid decline. Horgrim's theology is straightforward: Magic is a tool used to enforce the law of might upon all. Some scholars use ancient references to Horgrim as a god of magic and darkness to support the claim that Horgrim's role as a war-god is a secondary result of this theology. Any modern priests or worshippers of Horgrim must practice their faith in secrecy because there are no known active temples. According to ancient texts, worship services included a gathering at dusk and a simple, unified chant of, "Power shall bring the darkness that makes all equal before Horgrim." At the height of their power, Horgrim's worshippers counted many wizards, warriors, and nobles among their number. Many of Horgrim's priests studied wizardry and warfare to better serve their god. Priests and wizards led the many wars Horgrim's followers fought to expand his domain and were usually seen at the front of the battle line. Sketchy records indicate the priests and followers of Horgrim created a number of powerful relics that are lost or forgotten. The few existing relics that can be traced back to Horgrim's worshippers are powerful enough to lend credence to these rumors.

The Guardians

Any creature entering the mountain is watched carefully by the few guardians that remain. After a few minutes, one of the **couatl** guarding the temple approaches the characters to determine their purpose. The main remaining guardian for the cavern is Souref, an ancient **couatl** (with maximum hit points and increase Challenge to 8, adding +1 to attack rolls, ability score checks, and saving throws), who is supported by two younger **couatl** named Shiviec and Rivarn. Any of these creatures is a formidable opponent; all three together are particularly deadly. All of them possess gold tattoos embedded into the scales of their chest that they can activate at will with a number of special effects as described below. Shiviec and Rivarn are a mated pair and are always found together. If only one is seen, the other is usually hiding nearby. Souref is often encountered alone, but the other two are always close enough to rapidly come to his aid.

Description and Personality: Souref is a large serpent with feathered wings. Age has deepened the bright colors of his wings rather than fading them, making him even more colorful than the young couatl that assist him. Souref is vain, confident in his strength, beauty, and faith to Arn. Souref provides healing to those in need, but only if asked properly. Souref is resolute in his duty to prevent evil creatures from leaving the temple, and to keep evil magical items from being taken from it. In all the years here, he has only had two major battles. One with a creature that tried to flee the temple, and another with adventurers who entered the cavern with "evil hearts." Nothing would please him more than destroying some of the evil artifacts hidden in the temple, though he isn't even certain what those items might be. In the past 1000 years, he has witnessed three groups enter the temple. Two groups never emerged; the third fled the temple, bloody and terrified. Even after being healed, those adventurers decided against trying to enter the temple again. Souref would love to destroy any evil items the characters find during their exploration. Characters who willingly surrender powerful evil items for destruction might receive an item from Souref's treasure chest (See **Area D**) as a reward.

Description and Personality: Shiviec and Rivarn are a mated pair, though it appears that only couatl can tell them apart. The beautiful creatures joined Souref in guardianship of the temple approximately 50 years ago. They are far more playful, friendly, and outgoing than their elder counterpart, but possess less knowledge about the temple. Compliments on their beauty appeals to their vanity and makes them far more receptive to requests for aid.

General Tactics: As guardians, the couatl must prevent evil creatures from leaving the temple and prevent the removal of powerful, evil items. They have nothing against adventurers entering the temple or taking the treasures hidden within, but their oaths force them to attack any creatures identified as evil. All of them cast *detect evil and good* before greeting any new creatures in the cavern. If they believe it might help them to learn more about the newcomers, they use their change shape ability to adopt a human or elven form. They ask the characters why they have come to the cavern and how they knew about it. If asked, the couatl provide most of the background information on the temple, but this knowledge is told from the perspective of Arn's followers and is heavily biased. If the couatl trust the characters' intention, they welcome them to the cavern and tell them they can do whatever they want in the temple so long as they do not remove any evil relics or artifacts from the mountain; such items must be destroyed. Each time the characters prepare to leave the cavern after exploring the temple, one of the couatl activates its *detect thoughts* tattoo and questions them again. This time they just want to ensure that the characters are not leaving with any evil-aligned, powerful magic items. If the characters say they do not know, or are uncertain, the couatl ask them to show all the items they recovered, promising they can keep any non-evil items. A lie results in a request to empty their backpacks; if the characters do not comply, all three couatl attack.

Magical Tattoos

Powerful tattoos inscribed into the scales on the couatls' chests provide them with additional powers. An ancient process handed down through generations of couatl serving Arn is used to create the tattoos. While a couatl with the proper knowledge could inscribe these tattoos on another being, the magic is keyed specifically to the couatl physiology. There are five tattoos. The first, a sun rising over a mountain, gives a permanent resistance to *banishment* and similar spell affects forcing outsiders to leave a particular plane of existence. The remaining four tattoos can be activated once per day as a bonus action and provide the following spell effects: *wall of ice, haste, protection from evil and good,* and *protection from energy.*

Tactics: The magic tattoos (see sidebox) prevent *banishment* or similar attacks from working on the couatl. The couatl generally consider physical combat beneath them and depend heavily on their spells to soften up their opponents before risking their beautiful bodies and plumage in physical combat. The first action any couatl takes when going into battle is to activate its *haste* tattoo, followed by activating its *energy protection* tattoo. Shiviec and Rivarn use *wall of ice* tattoos to trap the characters. If this doesn't work, they close in for actual melee combat only if they have to. With all of his age and wisdom, Souref is far less forgiving than the younger couatl. Souref believes his actions are necessary for protecting the world outside the mountain and, after using the *haste* and *protection from energy* tattoos, wades into combat. In the unlikely event that one of the other two couatl is in trouble, Souref casts *sanctuary* on himself while he makes new plans.

Note: A fight with the couatl at the characters' present level is almost certain suicide. If the characters end up in a fight and realize this, they should be given one opportunity to drop their weapons and surrender. In the event the characters actually manage to defeat these creatures, they should receive a 10% experience bonus due to the added abilities granted by the magical tattoos.

Map 5:
Arn's Moutain
1 Square - 100 Feet
A
B
C
D
E
Temple
N
S
E
W
Major Cave Entrances
100 Feet above Cavern Floor

Keyed Locations

Several locations inside the hollow mountain are potentially dangerous. The couatl warn the characters of the more dangerous locations if they are treated politely. If the characters are rude, or if the couatl don't trust them, the couatl don't give the characters any warnings. They fly high into the air and watch how the characters work their way through any problems.

A. Tiger Lord's Lair

A stand of large trees surrounds an obvious home for an extremely large animal. A **tiger lord** (see **Appendix B**) made its way inside the mountain while traveling as a druid's companion. The druid visited Souref, and the tiger lord decided it wanted to stay and play so the druid left it here. A collar around the massive beast's neck allows it to shrink itself enough to climb up one of the exits when food inside the mountain becomes scarce. The creature is intelligent enough to avoid armored characters, but defends the small, tree-shaded area that it considers home. The tiger is a source of potential problems toward the end of the adventure. If the characters staked horses or pack animals outside the mountain someplace, it is very likely the tiger kills and eats them if they aren't protected somehow.

Tactics: Generally, the tiger lord doesn't attack anyone unless its home is invaded. If the tiger lord does feel a need to fight, it pounces on the most lightly armored character (it learned once before that metal doesn't taste good) and tears at them until dead. It is intelligent enough to flee if badly injured. It is also intelligent enough to guess that adventurers might leave something tasty to eat outside the mountain. If it notices adventurers inside the mountain, it climbs out to scout for an easy meal. The tiger lord eats one unattended horse or pack animal per week (chosen randomly), leading to potential problems when the characters want to leave. If Uvear (see **Area G**, Wilderness) is guarding the pack animals, the tiger lord leaves them alone. The characters can communicate with it if they choose, but it is very wary of them and unwilling to be anyone's companion.

B. Murder creepers

Numerous vines crawling across the rocks and bushes surround a small pool of water. Two of these vines are **murder creepers** (see **Appendix B**) that wait for thirsty victims.

Tactics: The vine waits patiently for prey to approach the water before attempting to grab it. A few small animal corpses hidden beneath the leaves and vines in the area mark the roots of the plant (can be spotted with a DC 13 Wisdom [Perception] check).

C. Peaceful Pool

A slow trickle of water flows from the ceiling high above to splash into a peaceful pool of water. Vines cover several stone benches looking over the pool as well as several small statues. Clearing the vines away from the statues reveals stone figures of men and women with robes and staves facing toward the water. The entire area is considered *hallowed* ground due to the many rituals and spells performed upon it by the clerics and paladins of Arn. This area is an excellent place to rest, heal, and plan.

D. Souref's Cave

Souref lives in this small cave near the top of the hollow mountain. The cave is difficult to detect (can be spotted with a DC 18 Wisdom [Perception] check) due to the magical sunlight pouring down from the ceiling and can be reached only with a *fly* or *levitate* spell, or some other means of flight. Souref is profoundly insulted if anyone enters the cave without an invitation and resorts to violence to expel them (see statistics above). Even Shiviec and Rivarn call to him from outside the cave and wait for an invitation before entering.

Permanent *daylight* spells along the ceiling of the small cave provide steady light. A small altar dedicated to Arn faces east, but no other furniture is in the room. Beneath the altar is a heavy wooden chest (unlocked, no traps) that contains a vast array of items collected over the years by Souref and his predecessors.

Treasure: The chest contains more than 100,000 gp worth of various gems and coins, and a number of magical weapons, armor, and other items: *boots of speed, boots of levitation, boots of elvenkind, cloak of the bat, cloak of elvenkind*, and a *robe of useful items*.

If the characters voluntarily turn over evil-aligned items such as *The White Eye* and *amulets of the dark sun*, Souref rewards them with a few items from his treasure chest. Choose items that fit the classes and levels of the characters and the power level of the campaign.

E. Shiviec and Rivarn's Lair

The mated couatl have a small home here that is usually used only for short rests and private time. The smooth-walled cave is 600 feet above the floor of the hollow mountain and requires some means of flight to reach. Nothing of value is stored here because the pair gives any items they discover to Souref to store in his cave. Couatl are intensely private with regard to their homes; any invasion of this home results in attack.

F. The Temple

The temple to Horgrim is detailed in the next chapter.

Chapter Eight: Horgrim's Temple Level 1

The massive temple stands in the southwest portion of the vast, hollow mountain. Each of its four sides is exactly 300 feet or was when it was first constructed. Three tiers rise above the temple, each much smaller than the last, before finally reaching a pyramid-shaped top. Each tier is approximately 30 feet tall, with the final pyramid at the top measuring 60 feet in every direction. While the stone building is ancient, the engineering and construction were extremely skilled. Horgrim's faithful hollowed out the mountain to create a nice, dark place to build a grand temple dedicated to the god of war and darkness. Although Horgrim's faithful lost the hollow mountain to forces of the good gods long ago, the sturdy temple remains unconquered. Outer walls of the lower portions of the temple are 20 feet thick, only thinning to 10 feet or less toward the top of the temple. Various minerals contained in the stone prevent scrying in or out of the temple, interfere with all divination spells, and make *passwall* spells half as effective as normal. In addition, the minerals in the stone make it resistant to *stone shape* and similar spells that shape or change the nature of stone. These spells are only half as effective in terms of volume and duration. The thickness of the walls combined with the strange nature of the stone makes using spells to create an entrance to the temple extremely difficult but not impossible.

Keyed Locations

The Doors to the Temple

Three doors are evenly spaced along the base of each face of the temple, with the central door always being a set of double doors. Only one of the 12 doors leads deeper into the temple and allows access to other levels; some of the other doors lead to other regions of the first level and contain various treasures and keys that make entering the higher levels of the temple somewhat easier. Several doors are simply traps, while others lead to rooms that are cleverly designed traps, or both. Numbering of the doors and rooms starts in the northwest corner on the western side of the temple and continues around the temple in a clockwise direction. All upper tiers are completely devoid of any type of windows or doors, leaving these 12 doors as the only visible entrances.

1. Iron Door

The humid air has added a patina of rust to the solid door. It is unlocked and opens easily.

2. Room of Broken Stone

Broken rocks cover the floor, all of them clearly from the ceiling above. This room was designed as a trap, with the ceiling designed to collapse on anyone attempting to pass through the room. Many years ago, several unfortunate adventurers fell victim to the trap, leaving only their broken bones behind as a testament to their failure. A thorough search of the room finds remains from at least 5 individuals, but no treasure. Narise (see **Area 3**) looted these corpses years ago and then moved the rubble back over the bodies. Dust covers a small open area before the door in the west wall. Someone took the time to move the rubble away from the door to open it, but dust coating the floor shows nobody has been here for a very long time.

A careful search through the rubble (and a successful DC 15 Wisdom [Perception] check) locates the trigger mechanism used to collapse the ceiling. While the trap has already been triggered, identifying this mechanism gives a character advantage to spot similar traps on this level.

3. Narise's Greeting Chamber

Flickering lamps shed a shadowy, uneven light throughout the beautifully decorated room. Velvet-covered sofas and chairs surround mahogany tables. Delicate tapestries depicting bloody battles decorate the walls, and a soft rug covers the floor. All of the items in the room have an air of great age yet are clearly cared for. One of the tapestries on the southern wall conceals a series of evenly spaced holes that Narise (female **vampire**) travels through in gaseous form to reach her special burial chamber (**Area 4**). The wall is 3 feet thick (AC 15, 45 hit points per 5-foot cube) and must be broken down or passed through using *gaseous form* or *passwall* spells. Narise uses this room as her "greeting chamber" when she is fortunate enough to have victims to toy with. There haven't been any visitors in centuries, so Narise generally keeps up this room and patrols the halls (**Areas 41–47**). If the characters haven't met Narise in **Areas 41–47**, they definitely meet her here.

Personality: Narise was a vain sorceress who accepted vampirism as a way to preserve her beauty and serve Horgrim as a guardian for the temple and the treasures hidden within it. She did not know she would be given what she feels is a relatively minor and immensely boring job. She knows a bit about the design of the temple, but next to nothing about the treasures it was built to guard. She enjoys using her powers to confuse and trick people, and relishes destroying good clerics and paladins. The first few decades brought occasional explorers and adventurers, but since that time, Narise has had few visitors and is bored and restless. She desires companions to spend her time with and gets very excited at the prospect of finding, or creating, some.

Tactics: Noise in either **Area 2** or **Area 5** alerts Narise to possible visitors. Narise is vain and overconfident, but not foolish. She greets the party in a friendly manner, joking with them by saying such things as "I keep telling you people I don't want to be rescued." Then she plays along with whatever presumptions the characters make. While she talks to the party, she looks for characters bearing holy symbols that might indicate clerics or paladins. Her first aggressive action is to attempt to use her charm ability on the most heavily-armed fighter in the party. She continues attempting to charm other characters until she is noticed, at which point she promptly moves away from the party and prepares for battle. The following round, she uses children of the night to summon allies. She uses any charmed characters to defend her by having them attack their friends. She does her best to stand back and enjoy the battle, casting periodic spells to increase the chaos of the area. If the characters overcome her charm ability, she enters melee combat with the character she considers most dangerous, usually a cleric, paladin, or elven character. Narise is bold, but not foolish; if she is brought to fewer than 20 hp, she assumes mist form and flees through cracks in the wall to her special burial chamber.

4. Sealed Chamber

Narise has her coffin here as well as all her special treasures. Her special burial chamber was constructed with narrow gaps and cracks in the 3-foot-thick stone walls (AC 15, 45 hit points per 5-foot cube) between **Areas 3** and **45**, allowing her to act as a guardian for those portions of the temple. The walls in those locations must be broken down or breached with *passwall* or *gaseous form* spells to reach the chamber. If the characters somehow enter this room without already meeting Narise, she is drawn back to her chamber within 1d4 rounds by the noise they make. Narise attacks anyone in her private chamber, using all her spells and abilities as described in the tactics section of **Area 3**.

Narise rests in a stone coffin (18 in. thick; AC 15, 55 hit points; DC 18 Strength [Athletics] check required to move the lid). While she does store some of her treasure in the massive chest at the foot of the coffin, the main items are in a hollow chamber beneath the coffin. A careful search of the coffin reveals holes along the bottom. Narise passes through the holes in gaseous form to obtain or store items.

Treasure #1: The chest contains a black velvet cloak decorated with small diamonds (800 gp), 3 hats of various styles (45 gp each), and a collection of silk scarves (30 gp each) that cover small bags with the following treasure: a gold bracelet studded with six diamonds (2000 gp), an emerald pendant on a gold chain (600 gp), an ornate silver bracelet (400 gp), and three ivory tubes filled with 250 gp of diamond dust each.

Treasure #2: A DC 20 Strength check is required to move the coffin aside and get to the primary stash of treasure containing a *+1 longsword*, a *rope of climbing*, and a *potion of heroism*.

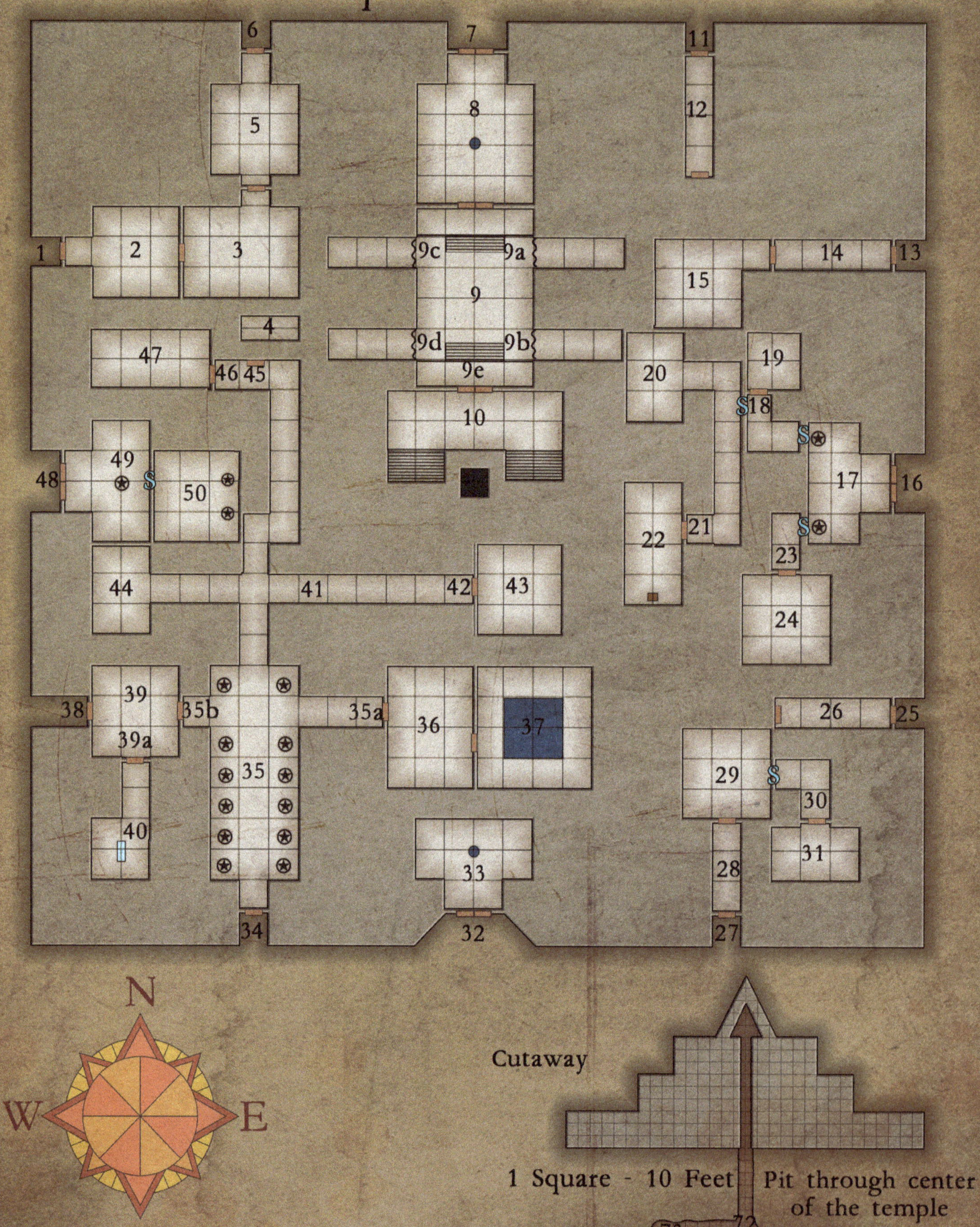

Map 6: Horgrim's Temple
1 Square - 10 Feet
6
7
11
5
8
12
1
2
3
9c
9a
14
13
15
4
47
46 45
9d
9b
9e
20
19
18
49
10
50
17
16
48
22
21
23
44
41
42
43
24
38
39
35b
35a
36
37
26
25
39a
29
35
30
40
33
31
28
27
34
32
N
W
E
S
Cutaway
1 Square - 10 Feet
Pit through center
of the temple
73
72

5. THE RED PATH

Red stepping-stones create a winding path leading through the room from the northern door (**Area 6**) to the southern door with a large, flat red stone before each door. Faded tile mosaics decorate the walls with pictures of rocky hills and strange, twisted forests. Approximately 20 holes line the walls of the room at a height of 3 feet. Almost anyone glancing into the room (Spot check DC 5) easily determines the holes are part of some sort of dart or arrow trap. A desiccated corpse in the center of the room provides another hint of danger. But what actually triggers the trap? A character examining the stepping-stones easily ascertains the red stepping-stones are linked to some sort of mechanical mechanism. What is not obvious is the fact that the red stepping-stones prevent the firing of darts while people are in this room. The entire floor, including the stepping-stones, is a weight-sensing mechanism that controls the firing of darts through holes in the wall. As long as one person stands on a red stepping-stone, the darts do not fire. If anyone is in the room without someone standing on a red stepping-stone, the darts fire at a rate of 20 per round. While the trap is difficult to disable, it is easy to avoid once the triggering mechanism is understood.

Dart Trap
Mechanical Trap

This trap is triggered when any creature is standing in the room and no creatures are standing on the red stepping-stones. The trap can be spotted with a successful DC 15 Wisdom (Perception) check and disabled with a set of thieves' tools and a successful DC 18 Dexterity check. If activated, the trap shoots darts at any character in the room, hitting with a +8 bonus and inflicting 4 (1d4 + 2) piercing damage on any hit.

Note: An unsuccessful Wisdom (Perception) check leads the character to believe that the stepping-stones are a trigger for the trap rather than a mechanism to keep the darts from firing. The trap is extremely clever, but purely mechanical. After 100 darts (5 rounds), the dart-firing mechanisms are empty and emit only hollow clicks.

Treasure: A rogue began a solo exploration of this area several centuries ago, and now only her desiccated corpse remains. It is so dry that it turns to dust at the merest touch. The only items that survive are a gold amulet (350 gp) and loose coins totaling 32 gp, 45 sp, and 72 cp. The coins are very ancient; a successful DC 13 Intelligence (History) check determines the coins are approximately 750 years old.

6. IRON DOOR

Iron Door: 2 in. thick; (AC 19, 45 hit points; locked and can be picked with thieves' tools and a successful DC 15 Dexterity check).

The plain iron door shows no signs of rust but is clearly quite ancient. When viewed from the outside, scratches around the ancient lock suggest other people have done some "work" on the lock without the proper key. Characters who approach the door from the inside (**Area 5**) find the door easy to open. The locking mechanism is connected to the inner doorknob.

7. LEAD DOUBLE DOORS

Lead Double Doors: 10 in. thick; (AC 22, 90 hit points; locked and can be picked with thieves' tools and a successful DC 22 Dexterity check).

Enchanted to harden the lead and make the doors impervious to heat and magical attacks, the doors are resistant to magic as well as physical blows. This, combined with the complex lock, makes the room virtually impossible to open without the twisted lead key (**Key T1**) found in **Area 22**. When they are finally opened, the doors emit an ear-piercing squeal.

8. DARKENED ROOM

The lead double doors open to reveal a room full of dark, roiling mist. While the mist glows magically and seems horribly ominous, it is designed only to cloak light sources and make them ineffective. All light sources attract the strange, magical mist, with normal lanterns and torches so effectively cloaked that they shed no light whatsoever. Magical light sources and spells produce a shadowy, uneven light to a maximum 5-foot radius. The only features of the room include a stone fountain in the center of the room and a set of rune-covered copper double doors set in the southern wall.

The stone fountain (AC 15, 45 hit points) in the center of the room exudes the strange black mist. Mist pours from the extended arms of a tall, thin wizard to flow down his body into a basin surrounded by serpent-like figures before swirling out of the basin and spreading throughout the room. The fountain shows a variety of different magic when studied with the use of *detect magic*. Destroying the fountain stops production of the mist and the remaining mist fades within 8 hours, enabling the use of normal lights.

Copper Double Doors: 5 in. thick; (AC 22, 90 hit points; locked and can be picked with thieves' tools and a successful DC 22 Dexterity check).

These rune-covered doors are enchanted to harden the copper and make the doors impervious to magical attacks. This makes the door very difficult to open without the copper lion key (**Key T2**) found in **Area 43**.

9. LARGE TILED ROOM

Large globes of glowing light hover inches below the high ceiling and illuminate a large room coated floor to ceiling with colored porcelain tiles. The colored tiles form a mosaic depicting furious black dragons battling groups of poorly equipped elves. The central section of the room is approximately 4 feet lower than the 10-foot landings in front of the north and south doors. Small, low steps lead down from the north and south landings to the central room where four hallways appear to extend to rooms filled with weapons, armor, or treasure. Characters who enter the lower portion of the room to look down the hallways might notice the floor is covered with traces of white, powdery dust. Only a very knowledgeable alchemist (with a successful DC 18 Knowledge [Arcana] check) recognizes the powder as Zhilac powder, a compound that can be mixed with acid to produce a deadly gas.

The entire room is actually a very deadly trap designed to prevent invaders from reaching the silver doors at the south end of the room. Illusions cloak the hallways (**9a–9d**) and conceal a large volume of acid behind a magic barrier. The porcelain tiles are immune to the acid, so the walls and floor effectively contain the horribly caustic substance.

9A.–9D. ILLUSION-CLOAKED CHAMBERS

Illusions cloaking these chambers make them appear to be hallways extending to large rooms filled with weapons (**9a**), armor (**9c**), or chests of treasure (**9b** and **9d**). In reality, they are 10-feet-wide, 10-feet-tall, 30-feet-deep chambers coated with porcelain tiles holding a potent acid. Characters attempting to enter these hallways encounter a strange, flexible barrier that appears to be some version of a *wall of force* spell. Attempting a *dispel magic* on a barrier, or any physical attack with a weapon, automatically dispels the illusions and barriers on all four hallways and releases a sudden flow of acid into the entire central section of the room. *Detect magic* reveals a variety of different types of magic at the junction of each hallway. Spells such as *true seeing* reveal the true nature of the hallways, but any attempt to disbelieve the complex illusions requires a successful DC 18 Intelligence (Investigation) check.

Acid Trap
Mechanical Trap

Only glass, porcelain, or pure gold items resist the acid. Water, wine, or ale is useful for rinsing or diluting the acid. Medium-sized or larger characters standing near the north or south ends of the room can attempt to leap onto the higher landings and avoid acid damage with a successful DC 15 Dexterity saving throw; all others must swim or wade out of the acid. Those caught in the acid suffer 9 (2d8) acid damage at the start of their turn.

Poison Gas Trap
Mechanical Trap

The acid mixes with the Zhilac powder coating the floor to release a cloud of poisonous gas that fills the entire room within one round. Anyone still in the room one round after the acid is released must either attempt to hold their breath or breathe the gas. All breathing the deadly fumes must succeed at a DC 15 Constitution saving throw each round to avoid suffering the effects of a *confusion* spell. Victims recover after 20 minutes when removed to fresh air.

Once the trap is triggered, the southern door is very difficult to reach. The poison gas fades and loses effectiveness after 24 hours, but the acid remains a potent barrier that must be overcome. The silver double doors at the southern end of the room are covered with a variety of runes that pulse with a faint purple light.

9E. SILVER DOORS

Silver Double Doors: 3 in. thick; (AC 22, 90 hit points; locked and can be picked with thieves' tools and a successful DC 22 Dexterity check).

The silver doors are designed to be opened with an ornate silver key (**Key T3**) found in **Area 50**. Enchantments on this door are similar to those on the lead and copper doors above. Attempts to damage the door with spells or to unlock the door with a *knock* spell fail. The acid and gas traps described above are immediately triggered when the door is opened, if they have not been triggered already. Magical protections designed to prevent the triggering of the trap when the key was used faded several centuries ago. Any means used to open the doors triggers the trap and creates a barrier the characters have to overcome when leaving the temple.

10. WIDE LANDING

Twin stone stairways to the east and west lead upward to the next level of the temple (**Area 51**). The silver doors in the south wall can be closed to prevent any poison gas from coming into this room. There are no markings on the walls or stairways to hint at what might lie in either direction.

11. Simple Stone Door

Simple Stone Door: 4 in. thick; (AC 15, 26 hit points; locked and can be picked with thieves' tools and a successful DC 11 Dexterity check).

The lock on this ancient door is so easy to pick that it almost seems broken.

12. Hall Full of Rubble

Rubble from the collapsed ceiling lines the floor, making it quite difficult to pass through the oak door at the very end of the hall. Despite its careful framing and solid appearance, the oak door leads nowhere. The entire room was designed as a trap triggered by a pressure plate in the center of the hall. A careful character searching through the rubble with a successful DC 15 Wisdom (Perception) check locates the trigger mechanism used to collapse the ceiling. Although already triggered, identifying the mechanism gives the character advantage on checks to identify similar traps on this level. The rubble also contains the remains of the unwary adventurer killed by the trap.

Treasure: A careful search turns up skeletal remains wearing an ancient gold amulet shaped like a spider, and a decaying leather pouch containing 5 pp, 39 gp, and 20 sp.

13. Ornate Stone Door

Ornate Stone Door: 10 in. thick; (AC 15, 26 hit points; locked and can be picked with thieves' tools and a successful DC 18 Dexterity check).

Ornate engravings of hawks and eagles adorn the heavy stone door. The delicate artwork conceals the complexity of the lock used to seal it as well as the deadly poison needle trap the lock once contained.

14. Hall Full of Rubble

On the surface, this room appears to be exactly the same as **Area 12**. The trap, its trigger, and the collapsed ceiling are indeed the same, but the decaying oak door at the back of this room leads into another chamber. If the characters search this room, they find that the unfortunates that triggered this trap escaped, with rogues being as likely to locate the trigger mechanism as above.

The door is old, but still very sturdy. It is unlocked but opens out into the room. Several bits of rubble must be removed before the door can be opened.

15. Hall of Broken Statues

At first glance, the room appears to be full of rubble. Broken granite and marble statues — items where craftsmen failed to make their mark or cracked the stone with their chisels — line the room in uneven rows. Most of the statues are of wizards or witches, while others depict monsters or strange, warped creatures. Although the broken statues are of no value, a beautiful flute made of a strange black metal lies forgotten beneath some broken rock and can be found with a DC 15 Wisdom (Perception) check (*flute of the black sun*, see **Appendix D**).

16. Steel Double Doors

The enchanted doors are sturdy, solid, and so well constructed that it is easy to believe they were recently made and installed. Opening the doors releases a cloud of dried pollen from a pink lotus flower.

Pink Lotus Flower Pollen Trap
Mechanical Trap

When the door is opened, a cloud of blue lotus pollen is released, covering a 10-foot area outside the opened door. Anyone in this area must succeed at a DC 13 Constitution saving throw to avoid hallucinations and disadvantage on all Strength and Dexterity checks. The effects last for 1d4 + 1 hours, during which time the subject suffers disadvantage to disbelieve illusions of all types. The trap can be detected with a DC 13 Wisdom (Perception) check but cannot be disabled.

17. Gas-Filled Room

A thick, swirling gray mist fills the room. Strange static barriers in the doorway to the east and the secret doors in the northwest and southwest corners contain the mist. While these barriers contain the gas in the room effectively, they can be touched or walked through without any harm, giving only the vague feeling of static electricity. The wet, poisonous mist hides 4 **mummies** and two statues of wizards in the west corners of the room. Secret doors hidden behind each statue lead deeper into the temple.

The poisonous gas protects the mummies with its moistness while it weakens characters entering the room. Fire-based attacks and spells used in the room do only half damage. The gray mist also makes the use of ranged weapons and spells difficult as it prevents any form of vision beyond 10 feet. Creatures who start their turn in the gas must succeed at a DC 13 Constitution saving throw or suffer 9 (2d8) poison damage.

Tactics: The mummies use the swirling mist to help cloak their movements as they move up to attack. They attack any living creature in the room mercilessly until destroyed. Their job is to guard this room against intruders coming from any direction. They do not leave the room to chase fleeing characters.

Note: Although the mummies do not chase fleeing characters, the poisonous gas makes them much more dangerous and difficult to defeat. Characters defeating the mummies receive a 20% experience bonus due to their added turn resistance and difficulties caused by the poison gas.

Secret Doors: 2 in. thick; 20 hit points; found with a successful DC 20 Wisdom (Perception) check. Once the panel of stone is recognized as a hidden door, it is easy to open.

18. Before a Stone Door

The featureless hallway ends before a plain stone door to the north and a secret door in the west wall.

18a. Plain Stone Door

Although the door is unlocked, it has no handles or clear sign of which direction it opens. A short investigation quickly determines the door slides to the right.

18b. Secret Door

Due to a gap in the wall, this door can be found with a successful DC 11 Wisdom (Perception) check.

19. Shield Room

A silver shield rests on a pedestal in the center of the room and sheds a faint blue magical light. Large metal shields coated with red enamel decorated with the faces of snarling hell hounds line the walls. A *detect magic* spell reveals an aura on all the shields in the room. Touching or moving shields on the wall has no effect, but touching the shield on the pedestal or attempting to remove one of the red enamel shields from the room releases the 7 **hell hounds** magically trapped in the red shields. The hell hounds leap out of the red enamel shields and attack anyone in the room.

Combat Tactics: The hell hounds begin with a breath weapon attack and fight characters in the room first, then track down any fleeing characters using scent once everyone in the room has been killed or forced to flee. They fight to the death and track fleeing characters anyplace they decide to run. If the characters hide behind a closed door, the hell hounds repeatedly ram the door to knock it down.

Treasure: The silver shield is an exceptionally light *+1 shield* decorated with delicate engravings. The seven remaining shields are steel shields coated with red enamel.

20. Abandoned Storeroom

The large room has wide shelves and racks along the wall but nothing of value is in the room. This room provides a relatively safe place to rest if a recent opponent is not tracking the characters.

21. Heavy Lead Door

The hallway turns slightly before ending in front of a sturdy lead door. Glowing runes run all along the outer edge of the door and circle the strange doorknob in its center. Opening the unlocked door summons a **barbed devil** into the hallway.

Tactics: The devil is almost as surprised at being suddenly summoned amid the characters as they are. Its first action is to hurl flame. It then tears into the most lightly armored foe near it with frightening ferocity. The demon doesn't know why it was summoned and believes the characters are attempting to enslave it. It fights to the death, pursuing any fleeing characters to the limit of its ability.

22. Lead Room

The walls, ceiling, and floor of this large room are coated with enchanted lead that nullifies any attempt to use magic to see into the room from outside. The only item in the room is a simple wood chest (locked, can be picked using thieves' tools and a DC 15 Dexterity check) resting against the south wall. A **blood wight** (see **Appendix B**) stands in front of the chest, remaining motionless until someone enters the room. Characters remaining outside the room can study it and the chest from a distance, but anyone entering the room is immediately attacked.

Tactics: The sentinel was summoned from a distant world and placed here to guard the key hidden in the chest. It attacks any creature that doesn't utter the worlds "Darkness is truth" before entering the room. It initially stands in front of the chest but immediately charges the doorway as soon as anyone enters without saying the proper phrase. It is bound to servitude within this room until it is destroyed and, hating the servitude, refuses to communicate even with characters who somehow learn its command phrase.

Treasure: The chest contains an ornate lead key shaped like an eagle with a forked tail (**Key T1**) that fits the door in **Area 7**, an *amulet of the dark sun* (see **Appendix D**), a dagger bearing serpentine symbols engraved on the blade, an ivory tube holding 500 gp of diamond dust, and a pouch containing an adamantine ring shaped like a hell hound biting its tail, 4 rubies (600 gp each), 6 agates (200 gp each), and 7 small bloodstones (50 gp each).

23. Ornate Gold Door

The short hallway bends to the south to end at an ornate gold door. Glowing with a strange magical light and decorated with ornate filigrees and beautiful designs, the door appears far more imposing than it really is. The only magic on the gold door is the magic shedding the pale green light, and there are no traps. While the door appears to be made of solid gold, the interior core is made of lead and only the outer coating is gold. Separating the gold from the lead is costly, but the effort still garners a profit of 800 gp to anyone willing to remove the door.

24. Dourala's Room

Dust-covered velvet cushions line several long sofas and small chairs surrounding a single stone statue in the center of the room. The statue depicts a female human in ornate plate armor swinging a large sword with both hands. Her expression is an odd mixture of pain and rage and bewilderment that is so deeply detailed that the statue seems alive. A successful DC 13 Intelligence (Arcana) check quickly determines that the statue is a victim of a *flesh to stone* spell. Dourala, a faithful servant to Horgrim, was unknowingly turned into a statue in the middle of a battle. Certain that the forces of good would return her to flesh and provide them with a powerful spy, Horgrim's minions left the statue here.

If the characters return **Dourala** to flesh, use the statistics and tactics described in **Appendix B**. She carries an *amulet of the dark sun* (see **Appendix D**).

Tactics: Dourala is not particularly bright, but she instantly recognizes that drastic changes have occurred since the middle of her last battle. She returns her sword to the sheath on her back if returned to flesh and calmly asks how the battle is going, waiting to see what the answer is before she mentions which side she is actually on. When informed of the time that has gone by, she gets extremely upset, and becomes even more upset when she is unable to locate her lance or bow. Dourala offers to travel with the party a bit before going her own way. If the party accepts, she does her best to quietly sabotage them, attacking openly if she is discovered. Her skills are aimed at battle, mostly leading mounted knights on horseback, not delicate subterfuge. If the characters are suspicious or disrespectful, Dourala draws her sword and attacks. She does her best to damage the party and then makes a fighting retreat out of the temple to escape and find reinforcements.

25. Plain Stone Door

The featureless door has no visible knob but slides to either side when pushed carefully.

26. Short Hallway

The simple hallway appears to end at a warped oak door but is really a trap. Anyone stepping into the center of the room triggers a pressure plate that causes the ceiling to collapse.

Collapsing Ceiling Trap
Mechanical Trap

This trap is triggered when any living creature steps into the center of the hallway. It can be spotted with a successful DC 18 Wisdom (Perception) check and disabled using thieves' tools and a successful DC 15 Dexterity check. When the trap activates, the ceiling falls in. Any creature in the room must succeed at a DC 15 Dexterity saving throw or suffer 28 (8d6) bludgeoning damage (half damage on a successful save).

27. Ornate Stone Door

Ornate Stone Door: 10 in. thick; Hardness 8; 120 hit points; lock can be opened with thieves' tools and a successful DC 22 Dexterity check.

Carvings of lions and strange, twisted animals cover the entire surface of the door. Opening the door sprays everyone within 10 feet of the entrance with insanity mist.

Insanity Mist Trap
Mechanical Trap

This trap is triggered by anyone opening the animal craved stone door. It can be spotted with a DC 15 Wisdom (Perception) check and disabled using thieves' tools and successful DC 18 Dexterity check. A fine mist is sprayed over everyone within 10 feet of the entrance when the door is opened. Any living creature caught in the mist must succeed at a DC 13 Wisdom saving throw or suffer the effects of a *confusion* spell. Holding down the tail of one of the lions prevents the mist from being released.

28. Short Hallway

This hallway is identical to the one in **Area 26**. The hallway possesses the exact same trap as the area described above but the brittle oak door at the end of the hall is real. The door is unlocked and opens easily.

Collapsing Ceiling Trap
Mechanical Trap

This trap is triggered when any living creature steps into the center of the hallway. It can be spotted with a successful DC 18 Wisdom (Perception) check and disabled using thieves' tools and a successful DC 15 Dexterity check. When the trap activates, the ceiling falls in. Any creature in the room must succeed at a DC 15 Dexterity saving throw or suffer 28 (8d6) bludgeoning damage (half damage on a successful save).

29. The White Room

Hexagonal white porcelain tiles cover the walls, floor, and ceiling of the entire room. All the tiles are highly polished and free of dust, but the east wall is marred by streaks of dried blood. A *detect magic* spell reveals a faint alteration aura on the entire room, but the magic of the room is designed only to keep it dust-free. A secret door (can be found with a DC 15 Wisdom [Perception] check) is in the center of the east wall. Dried blood has caked along a few cracks in the wall, making the door easier to locate. Once opened, it reveals a short hallway with dried spots of blood along the floor and walls.

30. Dragon Scale Door

A strange door made from the scales of a blue dragon stands at the end of the hallway. Streaks of dried blood decorate the walls as well as the scales making up the door. A *detect magic* spell easily discerns a powerful magic aura on all the individual scales making up the door. A complex magical trap breaks the door into its individual scales and sends them flying through the hallway if the door is touched. Dried blood in the hallway comes from some adventurers who fled the temple several hundred years ago.

Dragon Scale Door Trap
Magical Trap

The door blasts its component dragon scales into the hallway, hitting any targets in the way when it is touched. The trap can be spotted with a successful DC 18 Intelligence (Arcana) check and disabled with a successful DC 20 Intelligence (Arcana) check (dispel DC 18). When activated, the trap attacks all creatures within 20 feet of the door with a +10 to hit and inflicts 21 (6d6). Five rounds after activating, the scales fly back to the door, making the same attack against anyone within 20 feet of the door. When it resets, the trap reforms the door, which is locked (can be picked using thieves' tools and a successful DC 18 Dexterity check, failure activates the trap) and magically sealed (dispel DC 18).

The trap is difficult to identify without touching the door and can't be disabled, but it is triggered when touched with any object. Clever characters might hurl an item down the hall, let the trap fire, and run down the hall to enter the room (**Area 31**). The trap is also triggered when touched on the opposite side, but the scales only blast into the hallway and not back into the room.

31. The Dragon Room

Dust covers the varied decorations and furniture in what is apparently a living room. The furniture and decorations have a dragon theme and are also made from dragon bone, scales, claws, or horns. Most of the items, while valuable, are heavy and difficult to transport. Included among the items is a small life-like statue of a red dragon (**red dragon statue**, see **Appendix B**). The statue is a magic construct made from bone and scale fragments from an ancient red dragon that imbue it with supernatural strength. It is a potent guardian against anyone daring to enter the room.

Tactics: While the magic and items used in its creation were potent, the dragon statue does not have a complex program. It attacks anyone who isn't wearing an *amulet of the dark sun* (see **Appendix D**) by breathing on them and swooping down on them to make bite and claw attacks. It is programmed only to guard this room and won't leave under any circumstances.

Treasure: The furniture is worth more than 5000 gp in a major city but would require a large wagon to transport.

32. Obsidian Double Doors

Obsidian Double Doors: 4 in. thick; (AC 14, 14 hit points, locked and can be picked using thieves' tools and a DC 18 Dexterity check).

The highly polished stone doors show no sign of age, yet the stone around them is clearly ancient. Though they do not glow with any obvious magic, any damage done to the doors "heals" magically within 24 hours.

33. Skeleton Warriors

The room is a strange and frightening sight to anyone opening the door. A collection of armored **skeletons** (armed with longswords and shields, clad in plate armor and thus AC 20) stand at attention in neat, tight rows broken only by a small fountain in the center of the room. The mindless creatures were part of the army defeated when the cavern outside the temple was lost to the forces of Arn. Unlike most such creatures, these stand motionless, waiting for orders. The clerics and wizards that once controlled them are long dead. The creatures act only if attacked.

The foul green liquid in the basin of the fountain looks and smells dangerous but is harmless unless consumed (characters must succeed at a DC 13 Constitution saving throw or suffer 36 [8d8] poison damage and suffer the poisoned condition for 24 hours; no poisoned condition and half damage on a successful save). A *purify food and drink* spell cleanses the fountain of the poison but doesn't change its murky nature.

Tactics: Designed as low-level troops, they respond only to orders or to being attacked. Skeletons surviving an attack of any type charge forward to engage their aggressors and fight with single-minded ferocity. Only their previous orders keep them in the room; they follow fleeing characters out of the temple despite the dangers they face outside the room.

Note: Despite their numbers, these creatures do not pose a significant challenge to the characters at their present level. If the characters choose to destroy the skeletons, their reward is 30 suits of plate mail worth 150 gp each (the armor is old and in very bad shape).

34. The Lion Door

The massive bas-relief of a roaring lion thrusting its head out of the door conceals the doorknob used to open it. One must reach their hand inside the lion's mouth to find and turn the doorknob. *Detect magic* reveals a powerful aura around the lion's head, but no traps are on the door.

35. Hall of Heroes

Six statues of armed warriors are spaced 10 feet apart along both the east and west walls with gaps left where hallways extend to the east and west. The 12 statues are carved from the same stone used for the temple walls. Craftsmanship and detailing on each of the statues is superb, with each figure standing in a heroic pose, haughty and confident in their skill. Statues on both sides of the room are identical and depict the following (moving north to south): a tall male human in full plate wielding a greatsword; a thin male elf in leather armor holding a bow; a female human in chainmail wielding a longsword; a female human in spiked full plate wielding a longsword; a male elf wearing leather armor wielding a mace; and a male human in scale mail wielding a pike. It is impossible to determine who the statues represent as there are no signs or messages describing them anywhere in the room.

A *detect magic* spell reveals a faint aura around each statue, but none of the statues is magical or animated in any way. When the characters look down the hallways running to the north, east, and west, they notice the east and west hallways end at stone doors (**35a and 35b**), and the north hallway continues through an intersection and bends in the distance.

36. Barracks

Back in a time when the temple had living servants, this stale-smelling room housed many of them. Long rows of beds line the east wall, separated only enough for a person to climb between them — with the exception of a larger gap in front of a stone door. Chests at the foot of each bed are thrown open and ancient clothing and bedding is thrown about as if a tornado or whirlwind burst through the room recently. Although the room doesn't appear guarded, one of the temple's servants was changed into **dark warden** (see **Appendix B**) as punishment when the battle outside the temple went poorly.

Treasure: When the room was abandoned, almost everything of value was taken, but a thorough search of the entire room turns up a platinum ring studded with moonstones (500 gp) and an ornate silver bracelet (250 gp).

37. The Bath House

Humid air scented with perfume fills the air as tendrils of steam rise from the large pool of water in the center of the room. Created as a bath house for some of the faithful servants serving the temple, the magic spells purifying the water and keeping it warm and clean still function. Sweet, warm air makes the room especially relaxing and pleasant. Steps lead down into the warm pool of water, welcoming anyone interested in taking a bath, and soft sofas and chairs surround the quiet, bubbling pool. Soft towels and robes hang from pegs on the south wall. Disturbing portrayals of murder adorn tapestries along the remaining walls, jarring the otherwise peaceful feel of the room. Horgrim confined an ancient **erinyes** devil known as Lourecious to this room for being overly ambitious and acting against some of his interests. Her confinement ends when she converts one good creature to the worship of Horgrim, a task made virtually impossible by the fact that not a single living creature has entered the room since she was placed here.

Tactics: Although the room is beautiful and comfortable, Lourecious has been waiting for someone to enter it for years and is surprised when someone does. Startled enough that there is no time to cloak her real form, she decides against the attempt. Making no effort to cloak what she is, she greets the characters in a friendly, charming manner. Her goal is not to slaughter the characters but rather their conversion to evil, particularly to worshipping Horgrim so she can be freed. If she convinces a good-aligned character to swear an oath of allegiance to Horgrim, she is free to leave. At first, she simply makes conversation, asking the characters how they arrived here and informing them she is "trapped by ancient promises" and would like to escape. She offers to assist the characters but claims she can't leave unless someone utters an oath "to return to Horgrim what he desires when Lourecious is done helping me." The oath can vary; she is trying to make the characters promise to worship Horgrim (what he desires) while making them think they simply need to return her to this room. Most characters are suspicious of any agreements with devils and are unlikely to make such a promise.

If the characters attack or refuse to swear any sort of oath, she gets frustrated. She flies to the farthest side of the bathing pool from the characters and pulls out her weapons. She orders any charmed characters to swear their souls to Horgrim and attack their companions.

38. Cracked Stone Door

Ancient attacks on the door left cracks and gaps that are now filled with dust and dirt.

39. The Mirror Room

Mirrors line all the walls and a glass column stands in the center of the room. The column glows with a faint, almost indiscernible light that causes reflections in the mirrors to act like swift-moving shadows that dart across the walls. The faint lighting is insufficient to create reflections the crystalline horrors can use to manifest themselves. Brighter lighting brought into the room creates such a disturbing series of reflections that many people become dizzy (characters must succeed at a DC 13 Constitution saving throw or suffer disadvantage on all rolls and checks while in the room). While the characters adjust to the many confusing images, the first characters to enter the room are attacked by their own reflections as 3 **crystalline devils** manifest out of the mirrors and attack.

Tactics: Once they manifest, the crystalline horrors attack any living creatures in the room without mercy.

Most characters quickly realize the attacks have something to do with the mirrors. While some might stay and fight the creatures, wise characters leave the room and cast spells into the room to break the mirrors or cloak them in darkness and thus eliminate the threat.

The magically hardened mirrors are immune to acid, lightning, fire, and poison damage. Extreme cold makes them brittle (vulnerable to bludgeoning damage) but does only half damage. The mirrors are vulnerable to thunder damage. The large mirrors are arranged in panels all along the walls. If the characters decide to use spells to shatter the mirrors from outside the room, use the statistics presented here as an average and make the three mirrors used to manifest the crystalline horrors the last to break. Characters attacking mirrors physically may use a successful DC 15 Intelligence (Investigation) check to determine which of the mirrors might be the culprit. On a failed check, or random attack, use random dice (1 on 1d12) to determine whether a horror's mirror is struck.

While all doors leading out of the room are unlocked, they are covered with mirrored glass on this side, making them difficult to locate (can be spotted with a successful DC 15 Wisdom [Perception] check). Shattering all the mirrors makes the doors visible, but also covers the floor with enough sharp, broken glass shards to make the floor difficult terrain.

40. The Glass Sarcophagus

A crystal chandelier sheds a soft magical light on an ornate glass sarcophagus that fills the small room at the end of the short hallway. Red velvet carpeting covers the floor and the raised stone platform that the transparent coffin rests on. Violet curtains on the stone walls highlight the transparent coffins and its skeletal inhabitant. The creature within appears to have once been an extremely tall elf with folded wings. Glowing purple letters along the one side of the transparent coffin read, "Huvarial, Arn's failed champion." While letters on the opposite side proclaim, "Even the brightest lights learn the power of the night."

Huvarial, was a great hero in her day, but her exploits are entirely forgotten now (a successful DC 18 Intelligence [History] check reveals her name and story). Huvarial was brought down in the battle for the outer cavern and dragged into the temple, causing despair among her supporters. Loss of her leadership was a major factor in the decision to leave the temple trapped in a cavern of sunlight. Unfortunately for Huvarial, she was not dead, only disabled. Horgrim's faithful brought her into the temple and changed her into a vampire before trapping her in the glass coffin. Years without sustenance of any kind has caused the vampire's body to wither and decay, leaving only a bare skeleton. If the glass is broken, undead flesh quickly grows over the body and a very hungry **vampire** rises.

Tactics: Her transformation into a vampire is already complete, with darkness and hatred completely consuming her nature. This hatred is aimed at anything to do with Horgrim's minions and the temple as it is at any living creature. With more time to assess her situation, she would certainly use more devious tactics, possibly even allying herself with the characters to destroy the temple. Unfortunately, she wakes up naked, and her armor and weapons are nowhere to be found. She has no idea that she was frozen in time and acts on her previous plans to exact vengeance on the next person she sees. Although she is alert and awake immediately, she blinks and acts disoriented as she looks around the room while attempting to use her charm

ability on the nearest characters. Unless attacked, she climbs slowly out of the coffin without speaking or responding to questions. She then stretches her wings and leaps up to the ceiling where she hangs with her spider climb ability and orders any charmed characters to attack remaining party members. She exclusively uses her bite attacks and stays in physical combat unless severely injured. Severe injuries lead her to fly up to the ceiling, where she hangs face down while attempting to charm heavily armored characters. Huvarial's resting place is in this room; she fights until destroyed because she has nowhere else to flee. If the characters flee, Huvarial makes plans to hunt them down. Huvarial is not familiar with the layout of the area, having only been imprisoned here; she uses great caution when searching the halls and rooms nearby.

Treasure: Unknown to Huvarial, her armor and weapons are hidden (can be found with a successful DC 15 Intelligence [Investigation] check) in a hollow chamber inside the stone pedestal that the coffin rests on. The hidden chamber contains the following items: a *+1 longsword* ("Light's Cleaver") with symbols representing the sun engraved on the blade and a *ring of protection*.

41. Dead End

The hallway ends at a wall bearing a lengthy message written in dark green letters, "Put faith in Horgrim's darkest night and pass through solid rock. The message refers to the fact that the wall is a *permanent image* (a successful DC 15 Intelligence [Investigation] check to see through it). Characters without sight due to blindness or complete darkness do not see the illusion and boldly step through it to continue down the hallway. Although it has other sensory elements, the illusion is triggered by sight. Someone feeling the wall while looking at it believes they are feeling solid stone, but if they close their eyes and continue feeling the wall, those senses soon fade, and the wall no longer seems to exist. Anyone looking down the hall with a *true seeing* spell sees only a long hallway ending before a copper door.

42. Engraved Door

Engravings on the copper door include a variety of complex runes and strange symbols along with the words, "In the end, only the darkness is real." A detailed representation of Horgrim as a tall human in robes holding a shortspear is engraved immediately beneath the strange statement. None of the engravings gives any hint how to open the door, which has no visible door knob or locking mechanism.

Engraved Copper Door: 2 in. thick; (AC 15, 55 hit points, locked but can be picked using thieves' tools and a DC 18 Dexterity check).

Powerful magic spells cast on the door give it some magic resistance, making it very difficult to open by magical means (spells such as *knock* fail 50% of the time). Various runes on the door must be touched in a particular order. A clever rogue can eventually determine the proper sequence through trial and error.

43. Copper Room

Beaten copper, complete with odd lumps and strange depressions, cover the walls, floors, and ceiling of the room. An insect-like **copper statue** (see **Appendix B**) with a circular head and eight legs ending in razor-sharp blades stands over a copper chest in the center of the room. The statue is a magical construct programmed to attack anyone not wearing an *amulet of the dark sun* (see **Appendix D**) and keep them away from the chest.

Copper Room: Copper on every surface of the room helps retain and magnify electric charges. All attacks inflicting lightning damage do double damage in this room, and any saving throws against an effect that causes lightning damage is done so with disadvantage.

Tactics: The statue has razor-sharp tips at each end of its powerful legs and uses them very effectively. It releases its electric charge at the first person to enter and charges the doorway to defend the room. A massive reach and the ability to use multiple attacks make it an effective guardian. It focuses all its attacks on the first person to enter the room, only spreading its attacks if someone attempts to sneak past it. The construct is programmed to fight until destroyed.

Copper Chest: 1 in. thick (AC 16, 18 hit points, locked but can be picked using thieves' tools and a successful DC 18 Dexterity check)

The lid of the small chest has an engraved description that is a mirror image of the symbols on an *amulet of the dark sun* (see **Appendix D**) that is part of the locking mechanism. Any *amulet of the dark sun* can be used to unlock the chest.

Treasure: The main item of importance in the chest is a delicate copper key shaped like a lion (**Key T2**) that opens the copper doors in **Area 8**. The key rests on top of a collection of 1500 copper coins, copper bracers with black enamel trim, a copper *ring of protection*, a thin copper *wand of lightning bolts*, a copper-tipped darkwood wand (*spell wand* of *lesser restoration*, see **Appendix D**), 5 golden yellow topaz gems (500 gp each), and 4 amber gems (100 gp each).

44. THRONE OF NIGHT

The hallway opens into a large room with strange, twisted engravings of skeletons and strange bone figures decorating every wall. A massive throne of pure black stone rests against the south wall, beckoning someone to sit in it. Polished and smooth, the stone is still somehow non-reflective and seems to soak up any light that hits it. Any character able to *detect magic* instantly discovers a vast, evil power emanating from the throne, a throne once used to help create undead to support Horgrim's armies. Anyone sitting on the throne risks a terrible fate.

The Throne of Night: This powerful item is imbued with terrible magic through numerous dark, necromantic rituals. Made of simple black stone, it soaks up light as easily as it does a creature's lifeforce. Dead humanoid creatures seated on the throne are engulfed in swirling shadows only to emerge a minute later with the flesh burned from their bodies as animated skeletons. Living creatures that sit on the throne must succeed at a DC 15 Dexterity saving throw to leap off the throne quickly enough to avoid the swirling shadows. Those who fail are engulfed in the swirling shadows and forced to make a DC 15 Constitution saving throw or die as the flesh and lifeforce are stripped from the character's body as they are turned into an animated skeleton. Success indicates characters escape the burning shadows, suffering only 17 (5d6) necrotic damage.

Destroying the Throne: (AC 17, 306 hit points); Characters recognizing the immense evil of the throne might decide to destroy it. Although not a true living beast, the throne does have its own defenses. Attacks against the throne release waves of electrical energy once every round (attacking characters within 30 feet with a +12 to hit, inflicting 17 [5d6] lightning damage to those struck). When destroyed, the throne explodes in a blast of raw energy with a 20-foot radius blast; characters must succeed at a DC 18 Dexterity saving throw or suffer 35 (10d6) fire damage (half damage on a successful save).

Treasure: Once destroyed, the throne leaves behind broken gems that were used during its initial creation. A patient wizard can collect 2000 gp worth of diamond dust, 1500 gp worth of ruby dust, and 1500 gp worth of emerald dust for use as spell components.

45. WORN TAPESTRY

A worn tapestry with a portrayal of a human riding the back of a black dragon hangs on the wall in the center of the hallway. The odd placement of the tapestry suggests something may be hidden behind it. Anyone searching the wall behind the tapestry (Search DC 15) finds long grooves or slots in the stone that appear to lead to an open or hollow area behind the wall. These grooves provide Narise (see **Areas 3–4** above) with access to these hallways using her gaseous form. She doesn't usually come through this hallway unless she hears a great deal of noise, or if she has recently encountered the characters. If Narise has already encountered the characters, or if the characters make a great deal of noise, there is a 40% chance that Narise ambushes the characters somewhere in **Areas 41–47**. In that instance, she forgoes any play and simply uses the battle tactics mentioned in **Area 3**. The wall between this section of hallway and her **Sealed Chamber** (**Area 4**) is 3 feet thick (AC 16, 180 hit points) and must be broken down or bypassed with *passwall* or *gaseous form* spells.

46. BRITTLE OAK DOOR

Although once a sturdy, solid door, this portal has become brittle through the passing of time. The unlocked oak door opens easily but has a rather interesting trap.

Alarm Trap
Magical Trap

Opening the door triggers an *alarm* spell that lasts for 1 round unless the words "Love Horgrim" are spoken. The trap can be spotted with a DC 13 Intelligence (Arcana) check and disabled with a DC 15 Intelligence (Arcana) check (dispel DC 18). While the alarm spell does no damage, it alerts Narise (**Areas 3–4**) that someone is in the hall.

47. ANCIENT ARMORY

Racks of greatswords, pikes, shortspears, and longspears are evenly spaced throughout the room. Although extremely old, the weapons are still in excellent shape, possibly because a **dark warden** (see **Appendix B**) watching over the room polishes and oils them continuously.

Treasure #1: Of the more than 100 weapons lined up in the racks, a number are excellent quality weapons: 10 greatswords, 8 pikes, and 12 spears.

Treasure #2: One cleric took the time to create a secret hiding place beneath one of the weapon racks (can be found with a DC 15 Wisdom [Perception] check) where he hid several "personal" items in a small leather bag. The decaying leather bag contains a pale green prism *ioun stone* (+2 Str), a flawless emerald (5000 gp), 4 fire opals (1200 gp each), a black pearl (500 gp), 3 violet garnets (400 gp each), and 9 bloodstones (50 gp each).

48. BLACK METAL DOORS

Black Metal Doors: 1 in. thick (AC 18, 55 hit points, locked but can be picked using thieves' tools and a successful DC 15 Dexterity check)

These plain black doors are made of a mysterious alloy that is so heavily enchanted that it defies identification. While the lock can be picked, the lead key (**Key T1**) found in **Area 22** opens this door as well as the double lead doors (**Area 7**).

49. SMOKE-FILLED ROOM

Thick gray smoke pours out of the room when the doors are opened. The smoke dissipates quickly when it leaves the room, but the amount of smoke within the room doesn't change. Bitter and dry, the harmless smoke causes a bit of coughing and concern. A large marble statue of a serpent-like creature with three heads stands in the center of the room surrounded by four brass barriers. Smoke flows from the braziers in a steady stream, filling the room with bitter fumes. Although the smoke is not poisonous, it reduces all forms of vision to a maximum of 10 feet no matter what form of lighting is used. In addition, it conceals a **mummy lord** that guards the room against anyone not wearing an *amulet of the dark sun* (see **Appendix D**).

Brass Braziers: These items glow with several types of magic when studied with the aid of a *detect magic* spell. Covering the braziers with a blanket or some other item stops the flow of smoke. A *dispel magic* cast directly on one of the braziers (dispel DC 18) eliminates the magic on that brazier and stops the smoke. Once the flow of smoke from all four barriers is stopped, the room can be cleared of smoke in 1d4 hours if the doors are left open.

Tactics: Once a faithful cleric of Horgrim, the mummy lord retains much of its prior knowledge and experience, making it a very deadly foe. It senses the characters enter the room and moves out of its strange coffin quietly. The smoke gives it extra time to prepare, so it takes the opportunity to cast *resist elements* (fire) and *bull's strength* on itself and then casts *desecrate* before finally moving into battle. It does its best to attack and destroy anyone attempting to use fire-based spells or weapons on it, usually attempting a *hold person* spell first.

Examining the Room: Other than the statue and braziers, the only other item in the room is a sarcophagus that stands upright against the wall directly behind the statue. The sarcophagus is the mummy's resting place, and a cleverly designed secret door leading into another room. Smoke in this room makes it extremely difficult to recognize this, but if the braziers are covered and the smoke dissipates, locating the secret door gets much easier (the door can be found with a successful DC 18 Wisdom [Perception] check, but all Wisdom [Perception] checks in the room while filled with smoke suffer disadvantage). The door is counterweighted to allow the entire sarcophagus and door to slide to one side without much effort.

50. SILVER ROOM

Flaking silver paint covers the walls, floor, and ceiling. Peeling paint and silver fragments on the floor suggest the silver was a late addition to the room. Standing on silver pedestals are 2 **magnesium golems** (see **Appendix B**). Each golem attacks as soon as someone enters the room. Only a cleric devoted to Horgrim wearing an *amulet of the dark sun* (see **Appendix D**) can command the golems to stop and freely surrender the fragment of the ornate silver key (**Key T3**) each carries.

Tactics: The golems approach anyone entering the room. If a cleric of Horgrim does not show a holy symbol and utter the proper words within two rounds, they attack, focusing on lightly armored characters first.

Treasure: The body of each golem is worth 3000 sp and the ruby in each golem's head can be broken into 500 gp worth of ruby dust. A single piece of an ornate silver key is embedded in the chest of each golem next to a reversed engraving of an *amulet of the dark sun* (see **Appendix D**). Placing an amulet into the engraving releases the piece of key. The two fragments fit together to form an ornate silver key (**Key T3**) that fits the silver double doors in **Area 9** (**Door 9e**).

Chapter Nine: Horgrim's Temple Level 2

The second level of the temple is quite like the first. The outer walls are 20 feet thick and both inner and outer walls are made of the same material. Rooms and hallways have no lighting unless otherwise stated.

51. Chamber of Faces

Twin stairways climb up to a large room. Bas-relief carvings along the walls depict elegant humans and elves standing at attention. Some of the figures wear armor, while others have on robes, but all the carvings are detailed to the point that each figure seems life-like. Strange symbols are painted on the floor using dark reddish-black paint. Any magic the symbols once possessed has faded. Each figure is a follower of Horgrim who volunteered to meld with the stone wall and await a priest to reverse the spells that placed them there. Unfortunately, the magic that kept their souls from departing failed long ago. A *dispel magic* (dispel DC 20) cast directly on a bas-relief carving has a small chance of expelling the body of the victim, but none of the carvings gives rise to a living being.

A set of ornate double doors is at the southern end of the room. The doors are unlocked, though one of the dark wardens described below does have a key that can be used to lock them.

The room is heavily guarded. Anyone climbing one of the sets of stairs is attacked by 2 **dark wardens** (see **Appendix B**) as soon as they reach the top.

Note: One of the dark wardens has a key to the double doors described above.

52. Hall of Honor

Small statues and plaques fill niches along the long, wide hallway stretching to the east and west. The hallway bends north at its eastern- and westernmost limits before ending in front of double doors.

53. Frost-Covered Doors

The hallway ends before a set of steel doors covered with frost. The rune-coated doors are cold enough that they are painful to touch.

54. Room of Ice

Icicles hang from the ceiling, which glows with an odd blue light, and strange ice sculptures dot the room. The room is so extremely frigid a creature that ends its turn here takes 2 (1d4) cold damage. The extreme, magical cold of the room makes fire-based spells half as effective in terms of size, duration, and damage. Thick coats of ice cover a set of steel double doors in the north wall, as well as all the walls. A huge **ice elemental** (see **Appendix B**) guards the room; it creates strange, twisted sculptures and odd ice carvings during its long, boring tenure.

Tactics: Before attacking, this creature attempts to communicate in its guttural language. Unfortunately, only someone using *comprehend languages* or *tongues* understands it. It was summoned here and bound to the room as a guardian. All it knows is that it is supposed to guard the doors against anyone who doesn't have an *amulet of the dark sun* (see **Appendix D**). The ice elemental is willing to trade the key to the north door in exchange for an amulet, which it uses to exit the room and return to its own plane of existence. The creature communicates very slowly and isn't very intelligent. By now, the characters are probably used to attacking rather than negotiating. It focuses melee attacks on one target at a time, doing its best to kill one creature before moving on to the next.

Steel Double Doors: 5 in. thick; (AC 19, 158 hit points, locked and can be picked using thieves' tools and a successful DC 22 Dexterity check). The door is magically shielded, and any spells cast on it fail 50% of the time.

Approximately 1-foot-thick ice (AC 15; 30 hit points) covers the doors and must be broken away to reveal them. Faint runes near the lock suggest that it has been magically hardened and enhanced. The extremely complex lock requires a special key (**Key T4**).

55. Shattered Room

Ages ago, this large room contained a variety of furniture, sofas, chairs, tables, but now only broken fragments remain along the outer walls of the room. The devastation appears to be focused in the center of the room where an explosion threw everything into the walls with such force that virtually everything is shattered and broken. A lich left to guard this room eventually went insane. Without spellbooks to study or a particular task to fulfill, he decided that his continued existence was no longer fulfilling. Using *passwall* spells, he was able to obtain his phylactery from its hiding place in the walls of the temple. He brought it into the center of the room and attempted to destroy it. This act instantly brought down Horgrim's wrath and set off a detonation of such force that the ceiling and floor show signs of melting and cracking. Even the walls show cracks where furniture was crushed against it.

Dwarves or other characters with stonecunning instantly recognize hints that stonework was done to close off a wide doorway in the northern wall. The stone that was used matches the other stone used to make the temple, but its placement, and the cracks that run through it, suggest there was once a wide doorway here. Followers of Horgrim sealed this doorway, once the main passage to upper levels of the temple, after losing the battles outside the temple.

Bone fragments from the several skeletons left behind to serve the lich are strewn about the debris, along with a few treasures. One important item is a twisted metal key (**Key T5**, can be found with a successful DC 15 Wisdom [Perception] check). Once an ornate silver key with delicate filigree around the outer edges, it is now bent beyond usefulness. It was designed to open the door in **Area 59**. A character making a careful study of the item can use information from the key to gain advantage on checks to open the lock on the door in **Area 59**.

Treasure: A thorough search of the entire room takes several hours but turns up a few worthwhile items: a number of small gems, including a star-cut ruby (2500 gp), a tiny emerald (1500 gp), 12 black pearls (apparently from a necklace, 350 gp each), 15 pieces of polished jade (150 gp each), and 8 moonstones (50 gp each).

56. Red-Hot Doors

Glowing double doors at the end of the hallway shed enough heat to warm the hallway significantly. The doors are searing hot — so hot that they appear close to melting yet are somehow resisting for the moment.

Searing Hot Double Doors: The doors inflict 8 (1d8 + 4) fire damage on anyone touching them and 3 (1d6) fire damage per round on anyone starting their turn within 5 feet.

The doors are made of a mysterious alloy enchanted to resist very high temperatures. Although the doors are unlocked, they open outward and must be pulled firmly (a successful DC 15 Strength check opens the doors).

57. Room of Fire

The doors open to reveal a room filled with darting flames and molten rock. The walls and floor are magically enchanted to resist the heat and the presence of a 1-foot-deep pool of molten rock that fills the room. The fantastic heat inflicts 5 fire damage per round on anyone starting their turn in the room, and anyone stepping into the molten rock is subject to additional 2d4 fire damage per round at the start of their turn. Overwhelming magical heat in this room makes cold-based spells half as effective in terms of size, duration, and damage. The large black doors at the north end of the room appear remarkably cool when compared to the boiling rock and flames that surround them. Unfortunately, an angry **fire elemental** (maximum hit points and +1 to hit, saving throws, and ability checks) is looking for someone to wreak vengeance on after being trapped here for thousands of years. The elemental does everything it can to slaughter anyone entering the room.

Tactics: The elemental has been trapped here for so long that it is mindless in its rage. All it knows is that it has been abandoned by the mages that initially summoned it here. Enough time has gone by that it has forgotten what its duties are, or how it might be able to leave the room. It can leave the room only if it is "released" by a priest of Horgrim or freely given a holy symbol of Horgrim. Even if the characters manage to do this, it is upset enough that it is unlikely to care. It attacks one character at a time, trying to burn them to a crisp before moving on to others.

58. Sitting Room

Elegant sofas and chairs are organized into several sitting areas. Despite its great age, the furniture is in excellent condition. Everything in the room is clean, dust-free, and in some cases highly polished. Niches along the outer walls hold small statues and figurines made of porcelain. **Skeletons** stand in each of the corners of the room. The four skeletons are not outfitted for battle; they hold serving trays and cleaning cloths, making them appear to be servants of some type. Depending on the actions of the characters, this room should be a safe place to rest and recuperate.

A small fountain is in the northeast corner of the room, but no water is in the basin. Cabinets along the west wall hold a variety of liquors and wines, and jars contain the desiccated remains of what might once have been food. Sealed bottles of liquor and wine are still consumable, but the rest is beyond rescue.

A set of ancient oak double doors in the north wall leads into another room.

Tactics: These skeletons are servants that haven't had anyone to serve for many centuries. They do not initiate combat but fight back if attacked. They silently serve the characters any liquor or wine that is specifically requested and simply ignore requests they cannot fulfill. If the characters make no aggressive actions against the skeletons, they simply stand in their corners, moving only to polish furniture or to clean the room.

59. Priests' Quarters

The opulent decorations and furniture of the room indicate it was once home to only the highest ranking and most loyal followers of Horgrim. Gold, silver, and a strange, dark metal were used to create a figure of Horgrim as a tall human holding a spear standing before a circle of complete darkness adorning the west wall. A total of eight beds occupy the room, each spaced close together along the outer walls, and each having a large wooden chest at its foot. Several chairs surround low tables in the center of the room, along with a single wooden bench facing the west wall. Rods along the ceiling allow the various beds in the rooms to be cloaked by curtains, giving the occupants some privacy. In general, the room has an air of a military barracks, albeit a barracks decorated with wealth and style. Four serving **skeletons** similar to those in **Area 58** stand in each corner of the room.

A slow, rasping noise — like the heavy breathing of a sick patient — comes from the ornate double doors in the north wall. The noise is particularly disconcerting because it appears to be coming from the doors themselves.

None of the chests in the room is locked but they give up few treasures.

Treasure #1: The unlocked chests contain various daggers, maces, morningstars, and various pieces of decaying clothing.

Treasure #2: One of the chests has a false bottom (can be found with a successful DC 15 Intelligence [Investigation] check) that conceals arcane *spell scrolls* (*blink, fly, lightning bolt,* and *fireball*) and a *wand of fireballs*.

Ornate Double Doors: 10 in. thick; (AC 19, 158 hit points, locked and can be picked using thieves' tools and a successful DC 22 Dexterity check). The door is magically shielded, and any spells cast on it fail 50% of the time.

The beautiful doors are made of an alloy of several different metals that gives it a rainbow-like sheen on a background of black. Enchantments add to the strength of the door and make it very resistant to magic spells. As the ornate engravings and decorations would suggest, the lock for the door is extraordinarily complex. The ornate keys fitting the door have all been lost or destroyed, except for the key found in **Area 55** (**Key T5**). While this key is also bent and broken, a careful study gives a careful character advantage checks to open the lock. Oddly enough, the breathing the characters hear comes from the doors. Several priests and wizards used a series of spells to trap a **horned devil** within the door.

Release Devil Trap
Magic trap

A *magic mouth* appears on the door and asks for the "password." If the proper reply is not uttered within 2 rounds, a **barbed devil** is released from the door to attack anyone in the area. The password is "wiyeth," an ancient term for darkness (can be recalled with a DC 18 Intelligence [History] check). *Detect magic* reveals a powerful magic aura around the door, and *detect evil* exposes a powerful evil aura, but there is no physical sign of a trap. The trap can be spotted with a successful DC 18 Intelligence (Arcana) check and disabled with a successful DC 20 Intelligence (Arcana) check (dispel DC 22 but doing so releases the devil and inflicts 24 points of damage on it).

60. Narrow Hallway

The double doors open into a narrow hallway that extends past a wider hallway only to reach a dead-end. A massive black circle made of metal is bonded to the stone floor in the center of the wide hallway immediately before a set of stone steps heading up to the next level of the temple (**Level 3, Area 61**).

Chapter Ten: Horgrim's Temple Level 3

The outer walls of the third level of the temple are only 10 feet thick but both inner and outer walls are made of the same stone as the rest of the temple. Rooms and hallways on this level have a strange type of lighting that enables anyone with low-light vision or darkvision to see perfectly. Characters unable to see under these conditions need additional light sources. Unless otherwise noted, all the doors on this level are identical oak doors (unlocked) decorated with a carving of Horgrim depicted as a tall human male in robes holding a shortspear in his left hand.

61. Small Landing

Wide stairs climb up from the second level of the temple to reach a small landing with wooden doors to the east and west. The south wall is decorated with a brightly colored painting portraying a tall human male in black robes standing atop a mountain with his hands outstretched as if giving a blessing.

62. Preparation Room

Various chalices, scepters, vases, and braziers rest on a long table in the center of the room, and a variety of jars line the shelves along the east wall. Open cabinets in the southeast corner hold a variety of black-and-red colored linen cloths. Even the uninitiated instantly recognize this area as a room for clerics to prepare for holy ceremonies. An open doorway in the north wall leads to another storage room, and a closed oak door is to the south. Anyone entering the room without wearing an *amulet of the dark sun* (see **Appendix D**) is immediately attacked by a **dark warden** (see **Appendix B**).

63. Storage Chamber

The door to this chamber was left open so long that it sagged away from the frame and can no longer be closed. Casks of scented oil, unholy water, and other liquids line the room, all obviously meant to be used in religious ceremonies and rituals.

64. Adoration Chamber

This massive chamber is organized like a large church, only there are no benches, just faint dark lines along the stone floor where worshippers are expected to stand. A large mirror framed with black metal stands behind a plain altar resting on a raised platform on the west side of the room. Several oak doors dot the north and east walls. Horgrim requires only simple services from his followers, expecting them to show their faith by their everyday actions rather than in ceremonies. These "adorations" usually took place at sunset and included simple statements of faith in Horgrim followed by a pledge to spread this faith in Horgrim followed by a pledge to spread this faith to all lands. The black-framed mirror was once used as a portal between this temple and another a great distance away. Several clerics and warriors faithful to Horgrim fled through the portal when their efforts here failed. Unfortunately, they fled to a temple that had already been discovered and defeated by Arn's forces and were instantly captured. Other clerics forcefully moved and deactivated the portal to prevent any further desertions.

A **dark warden** (see **Appendix B**) stands behind the altar flanked by 2 **lead skeletons** (see **Appendix B**). They attack anyone who dares enter the room without displaying an *amulet of the dark sun* (see **Appendix D**).

Treasure: The lead skeletons have been studded with a variety of valuable gems along their ribs, teeth, and eye sockets. These gems include 4 large rubies (2000 gp each), 18 small diamonds (700 gp each), and 12 small emeralds (500 gp each).

65. Room of Coffins

Simple stone coffins are lined up against the east wall. The unadorned stone coffins are the final resting places for the clerics and wizards that lived out their final days in the temple creating the traps designed to prevent the forces of Arn or any other good god from violating it. A thorough investigation of all the coffins turns up only bones; all those interred here were placed into their coffins completely naked.

66. Burial Chamber

While high-raking priests and warriors merited burial in their own coffins lined up in the **Room of Coffins** (**Area 65**), lower-ranking personnel merited simple burial in a stack of small stone cubicles along the east wall. Small stones cover each square hole, with only the empty spots left uncapped. Based on the number of stone caps, more than 50 people were laid to rest here. Additional openings reach the ceiling, adding another 20–30 places for further burials. As in **Area 65**, everyone buried here was buried free of clothing or belongings.

67. Small Library

Heavy stone shelves reach from the floor to ceiling all along the outer edges of the room, and several solid stone tables stand in the center of the room. A strange metal ladder with wheels at the feet and a guide along the ceiling allows access to books on the highest shelves. The dry room has preserved the ancient texts but left almost all of the parchment pages extremely brittle. Any fire in the room creates a horrible inferno as flames leap from book to book all along the shelves. Many of the texts describe tactics for warfare, weaknesses of certain ancient armies, as well as weather patterns and trade routes. Although the information in those texts is hopelessly outdated, their great age makes some of them valuable to some collectors.

A **lead skeleton** (see **Appendix B**) stands watch here. The high priest that stationed it here ordered it to attack anyone other than him, presuming he would be back later to change those orders.

Tactics: The jewel-studded skeleton ferociously attacks the first character to enter the room. Although not really programmed to do so, it makes its attacks immediately inside the doorway, thus restricting who might be able to enter melee combat with it. Once it tastes battle, it chases any fleeing characters until it is completely destroyed.

Note: Any fire-based spells used in this room destroy all the non-magical books.

Treasure: Prying the gems off the skeleton turns up two large rubies (1500 gp each) and 12 small emeralds (500 gp each). While only a few of the ancient texts could be considered collector's items, those 20 books fetch a total of 8000 gp in a major city. A very careful study reveals a book titled *Iliachoam's Beasts and Saddles* (see **Appendix D: New Magic Items**).

Map 7: Horgrim's Temple - Level 2

1 Square - 10 Feet

Map 7: Horgrim's Temple Level 3

1 Square - 10 Feet

Map 7: Horgrim's Temple Level 4

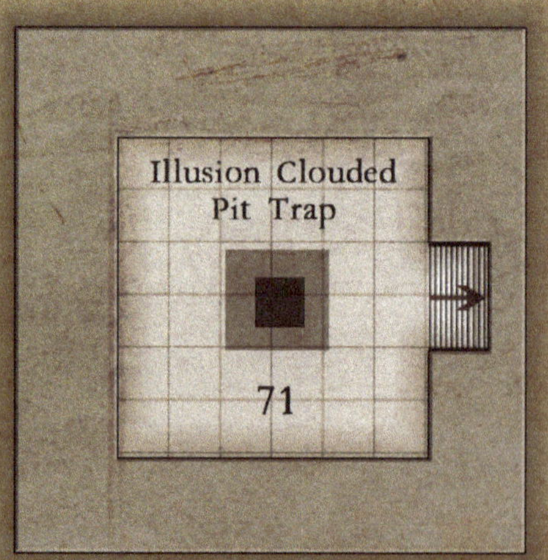

1 Square - 5 Feet

68. Small Library

On its surface, this room appears identical to the **Small Library** (**Area 67**). The shelves, ladder, and tables are the same. The books are quite different, however. All the books, whether mundane or magical, have bindings and covers made from scales of various types of dragons. All the mundane texts in the room are as dry and subject to burning as those in **Area 67**, but many of the texts here are enchanted against fire and other damage. These books include tomes of spells, texts designed to make shadow and illusion magic more powerful, and detailed discussions of Horgrim and the various spells and powers he offers his faithful followers. Perusing the texts is difficult, however, as the room is guarded by a **blue dragon statue** (see **Appendix B**).

Combat Tactics: The statue has a simple directive: Attack anyone not wearing an *amulet of the dark sun* (see **Appendix D**). When the door is opened, the statue takes flight and circles the perimeter of the room. It attacks anyone entering without the required amulet first with its breath weapon and then with its bite and claw attacks. Once the door is opened, the statue chases fleeing opponents. It is unable to open the door itself. If the door is closed, it simply returns to its resting position.

Note: Use of fire-based spells destroys any non-magical texts and stands a good chance of damaging or destroying spellbooks and other magical texts.

Treasure: The shelves are lined with a wide variety of books including non-magical texts worth a total of 2000 gp to an avid collector. Also, there are a variety of spellbooks that include the following spells: 0—all; 1st—*alarm, burning hands, color spray, comprehend languages, etch stone*, feather fall, mage armor, magic missile, shield, floating disc*; 2nd—*alter self, arcane lock, blur, darkness, detect thoughts, invisibility, knock, levitate, mirror image*; 3rd—*dispel magic, explosive runes, fireball, gaseous form, haste, hold person, lightning bolt, protection from energy, stinking cloud, suggestion*; 4th—*arcane eye, confusion, contagion, dimension door, ice storm, wall of fire, wall of ice*; 5th—*animate dead, passwall, stone shape, telekinesis, teleport, wall of force*; 6th—*contingency, programmed image*.

* The spell *etch stone* is detailed in **Appendix E: New Spells**.

69. Rune-Coated Steel Door

The steel door is covered with glowing pink runes surrounding a cloaked figure. Words engraved beneath the cloaked figure read, "Death is the entrance to new life."

Steel Door: 2 in. thick; (AC 20, 110 hit points; immune to spells such as *knock*, locked and can be picked using thieves' tools and a DC 22 Dexterity check); the door is difficult to open without the proper key (**Key T6** found in **Area 64**). Once opened, the door reveals a short hallway.

70. Short Hallway

Glowing runes decorate the walls of the short hallway as it approaches a small wooden door near its very end. Two **lead skeletons** (see **Appendix B**) guarding the hallway attack anyone passing through the steel door to the north.

Combat Tactics: The skeletons charge the northern door from the center of the hallway as soon as it opens. They attack with single-minded ferocity and run down any fleeing characters.

Treasure: Although the skeletons have no gems in their eye sockets, emeralds make up their teeth and tiny sapphires line their breastbones: 24 tiny emeralds (350 gp each), and 18 tiny sapphires (300 gp each).

The hallway ends before a simple oak door (2 in. thick; AC 14; 20 hit points; unlocked) in the west wall. Although unlocked, great age causes the hinges to stick slightly and create a vast amount of noise when the door opens. The noise announces the characters to anyone nearby. Once opened, a small stairway climbing up to the highest level of the temple (**Level 4, Area 71**) is revealed.

Chapter Eleven: Horgrim's Temple Level 4 and Below

Horgrim's Temple — Level 4

The bottom level of the temple itself is a single, very large room inside a pyramid. The walls are 15 feet thick and have strange white marble stripes that rise to the peak of the pyramid. The marble stripes are normal worked stone, but the main part of the walls is the same stone as the rest of the temple. Note that two chambers — accessible through the pit — lie even deeper than this level and are detailed below.

71. Bourafane's Refuge

Strange runic symbols cover almost every surface of the wall. Anyone making a successful DC 15 Intelligence (Arcana) check realizes these runic symbols are actually detailed descriptions of spells and not something left behind by a magic spell, or at least they were before they were defaced. Bourafane, a failed **lich shade** (see **Appendix B**) haunting here, used the very walls as his spellbooks. The eight marble stripes in the room each conceal small storage areas that can be reached only through the use of a *passwall* spell or by breaking through the marble wall (described below).

A single white stone with glowing purple runes stands on a pedestal in the exact center of the room, and a large throne-like chair made of bone set against the southern wall faces north toward the glowing stone. The glowing stone matches the description and sketches of *The White Eye* and the very peak of the temple would appear to be a logical place to store a powerful relic. Unfortunately, the glowing stone, its pedestal, and the floor beneath it are all permanent programmed illusions that are extremely convincing (can be disbelieved with a DC 18 Intelligence [Investigation] check). The illusions entice greedy raiders to step over a deadly pit trap and plummet 160 feet to a rough stone floor. A passageway at the very bottom of the pit leads to a room storing all the temple's treasures.

The complexity and skill that went into the illusions covering the pit make it very difficult to detect. *Programmed illusions* create a brilliant flash of green light emanating from the false eye along with a booming echo to make it appear that anyone falling though the floor has been disintegrated. Creatures that levitate or fly over the trap do not trigger this illusion. Creatures that attempt to grab the stone see it wink in and out of existence as if avoiding their grasp. Once identified, the pit is easy to avoid. Avoiding the trap also avoids the passageway hidden at its very bottom (**Area 72**).

Tactics: Bourafane was always a bit of a practical joker, something that may be highlighted by the constant loneliness inflicted on him the past few thousand years. Bourafane wants the characters to get the treasures they seek, but his promises prevent him from openly helping them. When he hears the door (**Level 3, Area 70**) opening, he rises, greets them in a friendly manner, and welcomes them to his small "prison." He waves a hand at the illusionary pedestal and stone and says, "This is what you are seeking. Please take it, but only if you are pure of heart." He uses vague terms to make the characters believe that the illusionary *White Eye* is actually a good artifact that was stolen and hidden here to prevent others from using it. Bourafane knows about the trap and the true treasure beneath the temple. If the characters are direct with their questions, Bourafane is forced to give honest answers, but he does his best to use vague terms.

Marble chambers: Only a clever individual realizes the marble stone might conceal storage spaces. The eight marble stripes that reach from floor to ceiling each conceal small niches that can be accessed only through a *passwall* or similar spell or by breaking through the stone (3 ft. thick; AC 16, 28 hit points each). While only three of the hidden chambers contain treasure, these treasures are worth all the effort involved. Bourafane considers all the items listed below his personal possessions. Bourafane attacks anyone attempting to steal his treasures and must be defeated before the chambers can be safely accessed.

Chambers 1–3: Empty.

Chamber 4: A black velvet bag holding 3 perfect emeralds (7000 gp each) and a blue diamond (5500 gp), and a leather bag holding 500 ancient gold coins (worth 1 gp each for gold value or 5 gp each to a collector in a large city).

Chamber 5: A diamond pendant on a platinum chain (*necklace of adaptation*)

Chamber 6–7: Empty.

Chamber 8: Several *figurines of wondrous power*, including a bronze griffin, marble elephant, obsidian steed, and an onyx dog. There is no hint of the command words for these items. Days of study and experimentation are required to learn the command word for each figurine.

Horgrim's Temple — Beneath the Temple

The final level of the temple is actually deep beneath the ground. The short hallway and room here are carved from the granite of the surrounding mountains and subject to all the spells that normally modify or change rough stone. Absolutely no lighting exists in this part of the temple; darkvision or a light source are required to see. These chambers are accessed by the pit.

Note: See the side-view map for the location of these room.

72. Bottom of the Pit

The rough stone floor and walls clearly indicate that the bottom of the pit is deep below the surface. Despite its rough nature, no debris is here, just a thick coat of dust from the surrounding walls. A narrow passageway runs west toward a large room.

73. The Treasure Chamber

Horgrim's faithful used this large room to store vast amounts of money and items to keep it out of the hands of their enemies. Numerous small bags are stacked against the three massive chests, each almost as large as a coffin, which are lined up against the outer walls. A **stone golem** shaped like a statue of Horgrim guards the chamber against all intruders.

Tactics: The golem attacks anyone entering the treasure chamber and continues its attacks until everyone is dead or it is destroyed.

Treasure: Traps do not protect the chests or bags, and all are unlocked. The total treasure trove includes: *The White Eye* (see **Appendix D**), 23 *amulets of the dark sun* (see **Appendix D**), a *cloak of arachnida*, and 60,000 gp worth of coins and gems.

Concluding the Adventure

After departing the temple, the characters can give the many evil items they find in the temple to Souref (see **Chapter 7: Arn's Mountain**) who destroys them and rewards the characters with several items from his treasure trove (your option, usually items appropriate to the characters' character classes). Souref considers the destruction of the eye a great and holy task and rewards the characters generously if they successfully obtain it. Treasure throughout this portion of the adventure is generally appropriate to the challenges the characters faced. If the characters missed some treasure caches, Souref can be used to make up the difference in items and wealth.

While the characters still need to return to civilization, their new wealth and store of magic items should make travel through the wilderness relatively safe.

Continuing Adventures

The baron and Ander Fierk are still alive and are now running from the king's men with accusations of treason, torture, and murder attached to their names. The characters might be hired to track down these criminals, or the traitors might begin hunting the characters to exact revenge.

Londar, once *resurrected*, goes into hiding and slowly rebuilds his power and resources before finally tracking down the characters and punishing them for their theft of his private papers and spellbooks. Alternatively, Londar might hire the characters to assist him.

Treasure in Londar's vault and in Horgrim's Temple include treasure maps and papers describing ancient ruins and lost artifacts.

Uvear, after being helped by the characters, asks them to help him find one of his clan's lost relics.

Major NPCs in Hampton Hill

Statistics and descriptions for **Learah Relight**, **Alfguir K'Eliek**, and **Ander Fierk**, the three individuals most interested in Londar's disappearance, are listed first, followed by statistics for other NPCs in Hampton Hill.

Learah Relight

Learah is a slight, dark-haired woman with a great deal of beauty and presence. Her aquiline features and violet eyes attract a great deal of attention. Her recent marriage to the son of a major shipping magnate has made her wealthy enough to dress in the latest styles. Though she wears a variety of rather expensive jewelry, the disappearance of her uncle has made her partial to the ruby pendant he gave her on her 16th birthday.

Despite some rumors to the contrary, Learah deeply loved her uncle. Londar was one of the few people who could understand the strange changes she went through as she discovered sorcerous powers during adolescence. Londar was also her only remaining family after her parents died in a carriage accident; he cared for her and helped her care for her family's estate. Learah desperately wants to know what happened to her beloved uncle and is willing to hire adventurers to investigate his disappearance. Learah doesn't care about Londar's money, but she does claim ownership of the spells and magic items Londar created, believing she knows what Londar would like her to do with them.

Although she has a key that opens several doors, she has no way past the golems guarding several of Londar's rooms, nor does she know anything about the traps he set throughout his mansion. Learah is disappointed with the sheriff and the town guards, and is actively seeking adventurers willing to help search for her uncle. Learah is satisfied that Londar isn't in any of the regular rooms of his mansion but hopes there might be a clue to his whereabouts hidden either in his office or his tower. She is happy to provide her key to the mansion to anyone willing to investigate Londar's disappearance. Although many doors the key fits have already been opened or broken down, possessing the key allows characters to demonstrate their right to search the mansion and to be in possession of Londar's things.

Learah and her guards have a suite at The Red House, and she can be found at The White Boar Inn every evening. When she hears of adventurers in town, she sends a message to them asking for a meeting at one of those locations.

Note: Learah travels with some expensive jewelry and clothing, so her husband sent three bodyguards (**knights**) with her for protection. Her jewelry is easy to identify and extremely difficult for a thief to safely fence.

Learah Relight

Medium humanoid (human), chaotic neutral

Armor Class 12
Hit Points 11 (2d8 + 2)
Speed 30 ft.

STR	DEX	CON	INT	WIS	CHA
8 (−1)	14 (+ 2)	13 (+ 1)	16 (+3)	11 (+0)	12 (+ 1)

Skills Arcana +5, Perception +2, Persuasion +3
Senses passive Perception 12
Languages Common, Draconic, Elven
Challenge 2 (450 XP)

Spell casting. Learah is a 2nd-level spellcaster. Her spellcasting ability is Intelligence (spell save DC 13, +5 to hit with spell attacks). She has the following spells prepared:
Cantrips (at will): *mage hand, minor illusion, prestidigitation*
1st level (3 slots): *charm, comprehend languages, detect magic*

Actions

Dagger. *Melee Weapon Attack:* +4 to hit, reach 5 ft., one target, *Hit:* 4 (1d4 + 2) piercing damage.

Alfguir K'Eliek

With an average height and weight and nondescript features, Alfguir blends into crowds quite easily when he wants to do so. His short dark hair has begun to gray at the temples, and a few wrinkles have etched their way into his rather bland face. Alfguir's brown eyes always seem to look away from anyone to whom he is speaking, darting around the room nervously as though he is searching for something. Age has slowed and weakened him, but he is still a formidable foe. Not many people know Alfguir very well — he appeared in town shortly after Londar's recent disappearance — but those who have met him in and around town found him to be polite, charming, and cultured.

Alfguir is a senior member of the thieves' guild, and he is the specific thief Londar hired to obtain a number of special items. Londar never paid him for his work, using his reputation and promises of new magic items to obtain "credit." Alfguir has an impeccable reputation and background as an honest merchant and is known to many other merchants and nobles. While his merchant business initially began as a cover story, he runs a true merchant house and does a great deal of legitimate business.

When meeting the characters or discussing Londar with others, he claims that Londar owes him a great deal of money, and he has excellent forged documents created by a master forger specifically to legalize his claims against Londar. Now that Londar has disappeared, there is no way to prove that these documents are forgeries. Alfguir plays up the act of a wounded merchant who lost a huge amount of money and is searching for someone to help him recover at least some of his losses.

Alfguir claims that his documents allow him to legally send in "representatives" to claim some of Londar's wealth, a claim supported by the local mayor and guards but that Learah contests. Although greedy, Alfguir is content to receive as much money as he can get, offering a "finder's fee" to the characters to hire them. If the characters investigate Londar's disappearance on their own or work for someone else, Alfguir attempts to use his forged documents to lay claim to some of their spoils.

Alfguir avoids any risk of exposing his true business. He hired other thieves through the thieves' guild to recover some of the money and items he feels he is owed, but so far, they have either disappeared or failed. Rather than risking more members of the guild and possibly exposing his true business, Alfguir decided to turn to hiring adventurers to do his dirty work. Alfguir does not know that the first group of thieves sent to collect money from Londar fought with him or that Londar died as a result of being poisoned in that battle. This means that he can conceal his involvement in Londar's death even if exposed to truth spells or potions.

Alfguir is staying at The White Boar Inn and can be found dining there every day. He is willing to contact and meet adventurers any place in town and at any time. He keeps his initial contact open, "honest," and aboveboard.

Alfguir K'Eliek

Medium humanoid (human), neutral

Armor Class 14 (wears studded leather and has AC 16 when "working")
Hit Points 40 (9d8)
Speed 30 ft.

STR	DEX	CON	INT	WIS	CHA
11 (+0)	19 (+4)	10 (+0)	14 (+2)	10 (+0)	10 (+0)

Skills Deception +8, Perception +8, Stealth +12, Thieves' Tools +8
Senses passive Perception 18
Languages Common, Dwarven, Elven, Thieves' Cant
Challenge 9 (5,000 XP)

Evasion. If subject to an effect that would allow Alfguir to make a Dexterity saving throw for half damage, Alfguir instead suffers no damage from the attack on a successful save, and half damage if he fails.

Poisoned blades. Alfguir doesn't fight fair. As a bonus action, he may apply a dose of poison to his rapier. His next successful attack with the rapier inflicts an additional 18 (5d6) poison damage and the target must make DC 15 Constitution saving throw or gain the poisoned condition until the end of its next turn.

Sneak attack. If Alfguir has advantage to attack a creature or has an ally within 30 feet of the target, and hits, he may add +5d6 to the damage.

Thieves' Guild Leader. Alfguir is the leader of a gang of cutthroats, bravos, and assassins. He always has 1d6 **bandits** hiding nearby and calls upon them to join a fight as a free action.

Actions

Multiattack. Alfugir makes two Rapier attacks.
Rapier. *Melee:* +8 to hit, reach 5 feet, 1 creature, *Hit:* 8 (1d8 + 4) piercing.
Light crossbow. *Ranged Weapon Attack:* +8 to hit, range 80/310 ft., one target, *Hit:* 8 (1d8 + 4) piercing damage.

Ander Fierk

Ander is a thin, dark-haired gentleman with an extremely pale complexion. His piercing black eyes and unblinking stare make some people nervous, while others find it comforting to know he is focused on what they are saying. Dark clothing highlights his pale skin, giving him an almost ghostly appearance that is enhanced by the magic cloak that billows behind him in perfectly still air. He carries a large travel bag containing spellbooks, spell components, and various other items that he is unwilling to let out of his sight. Ander is really the disavowed son of a major nobleman in a distant country. Ander has long-term plans of returning to his homeland with a small army, slaughtering his family, and carving out his own barony.

Several years ago, Londar and Ander discussed the creation of golems and other creatures out of stone. Letters Londar sent to Ander recently indicated he had found a method to create a stone creature that would be useful in battle. Based on prior agreements, Ander came to town to learn more. Londar's disappearance has triggered Ander's greed. Ander wants the spells he knows Londar created, as well as the methods to create his own army.

When Ander discovers the characters are planning to investigate Londar's disappearance, he approaches them and offers a great deal of money for the ability to copy some of Londar's spells. He presents himself as a simple wizard in pursuit of knowledge and offers a few potions as a sign of goodwill. Ander's offers of wealth are quite false; he doesn't really have any money to offer the characters. During his stay in Hampton Hill, he initiates conversations with Baron Kurell and eventually joins the baron, believing that is his best route to power. Ander has rented a small, private cottage to allow him to watch the characters through scrying and spying to determine whether they have found Londar's spellbooks and papers.

Ander Fierk

Medium humanoid (human), chaotic evil

Armor Class 11
Hit Points 58 (9d8 + 18)
Speed 30 ft.

STR	DEX	CON	INT	WIS	CHA
14 (+2)	13 (+1)	14 (+2)	17 (+3)	10 (+0)	13 (+1)

Skills Arcana +7, Deception +5, History +7, Nature +7
Senses passive Perception 11
Languages Common, Draconic, Elven
Challenge 9 (5,000 XP)

Spellcasting. Ander is a 9th-level spellcaster. His spellcasting ability is Intelligence (spell save DC 13, +5 to hit with spell attacks). He has the following spells prepared:
Cantrips (at will): *acid splash, mending, minor illusion, prestidigitation*
1st level (4 Slots): *alter self, burning hands, magic missile, shield*
2nd level (3 Slots): *dark vision, invisibility, shatter, web*
3rd level (3 Slots): *fireball, fly, hypnotic pattern, slow*
4th level (3 Slots): *black tentacles, confusion, dimension door, greater invisibility*
5th level (1 Slots): *conjure elemental, dominate person*

Actions

Dagger. *Melee Weapon Attack:* +5 to hit, reach 5 ft., one target, *Hit:* 3 (1d4 + 1) piercing damage.
Wand of fireballs. Ander possesses a *wand of fireballs* and is willing to use it.

Baron Kurell

Baron Kurell is a tall, thin man with dark hair and extremely pale skin. He dresses in robes decorated with his coat-of-arms and pretends to be nothing more than a nobleman that has studied wizardry on the side. He keeps his devotion and worship of Orcus a tightly held secret, hoping to someday reveal his true faith. He is a meticulous man, in both his clothing and mannerisms, and is extremely cautious. He keeps his raging tirades and penchant for torture carefully hidden from all but his closest advisors. The baron made an agreement with Londar that he never intended to honor. Unfortunately, Londar's disappearance came a bit earlier than he originally planned. Rather than trying to hire the characters directly, he throws his support behind Learah Relight's efforts to determine Londar's whereabouts. He mentions that his "dear friend" was researching a few items that some miners discovered near his home and is hoping nothing untoward happened to Londar or the items in his care. Acting as a family friend, despite never having met Learah, the baron encourages her to hire adventurers to search for Londar. The baron believes that adventurers motivated by profit are easier to control and deal with than guardsmen and hopes he can simply pay for or steal back the items he desires.

The baron makes use of *nondetection* spells when he is in public, knowing that he must conceal his true faith. While not terribly charismatic, he is a skilled diplomat and conceals his true motives extremely well. Enraged by recent changes to major trade paths by the young king now on the throne, the baron plans nothing less than a civil war designed to create his own kingdom and reassert his power and wealth through control of several different trade routes. Information received through visions granted him by Orcus helped him begin building a small army powered by several ancient relics. Added powers granted by *Horgrim's Pyramid* and *The White Eye* are all that he needs to tip the scales significantly in his favor.

Note: The baron has a suite in The Red House and is traveling with an advisor (**noble**) and three **guards**.

Baron Kurell

Medium humanoid, chaotic evil

Armor Class 18 (plate armor)
Hit Points 49 (9d8 + 9)
Speed 30 ft.

STR	DEX	CON	INT	WIS	CHA
12 (+1)	14 (+2)	12 (+1)	17 (+3)	19 (+4)	13 (+1)

Skills Arcana +7, Deception +5, Religion +7
Resistances necrotic damage
Senses passive Perception 14
Languages Abyssal, Common, Draconic, Infernal
Challenge 12 (8,400 XP)

Spellcasting. Baron Kurell is a 9th-level spellcaster. His spellcasting ability is Wisdom (spell save DC 16, +8 to hit with spell attacks). He has the following spells prepared:
Cantrips (at will): *guidance, light, resistance, thaumaturgy*
1st level (4 slots): *bane, cure wounds, detect evil and good, inflict wounds, protection from evil and good*
2nd level (3 slots): *darkness, hold person, moonbeam, silence, zone of truth*
3rd level (3 slots): *animate dead, dispel magic, magic circle, protection from energy, speak with dead*
4th level (3 slots): *banishment, control weather, fear, divination, vampiric touch*
5th level (1 slots): *contagion, contact outer plane, insect plague*

Actions

Command undead. As an action, the baron may hold forth his holy symbol of Orcus and attempt to take command of undead. Any undead creature within 30 feet whose Intelligence score is less than 6 must make a DC 16 Wisdom saving throw or gain the charmed condition. See Channel Divinity: Command Undead in the Undeath domain (**Appendix C: New Domain**).
Mace. *Melee Weapon Attack:* +5 to hit, reach 5 ft., one target, *Hit:* 5 (1d8 + 1) bludgeoning plus an 4 (1d8) necrotic damage.

Town Officials in Hampton Hill

Strybyorn Arthand

Strybyorn (male human **noble**) was once a very successful merchant and businessman but he has now taken to being mayor as his only job. He is in good enough physical shape that, despite his gray hair and wrinkles, people usually estimate he is in his low 50s. Strybyorn is actually 67 years old and enjoys his peaceful, quiet life. A quiet, friendly nature and disarming smile have made him such a trusted mayor that any thoughts of replacing him were forgotten years ago. His position as mayor makes him the sole judge for adjudicating disputes and for criminal trials. Although friendly and kind, he strictly interprets the law and does not hesitate to throw anyone, even nobles, into the dungeon if the crime calls for it. He knows that Londar's carriage was found overturned along the Horrik Trade Path and that several other bodies were found with it but turns any further questioning over to **Hamra Ranthas**. Strybyorn has known **Learah Relight** since she was a child and has a very high opinion of her, and he has done completely legitimate business with **Alfguir K'Eliek** in the past. He recommends both people highly. He met **Ander Fierk** one evening and had a long conversation with him. While he doesn't understand why Ander is in town, he found him to be a pleasant enough person. Characters who speak to Strybyorn at length rapidly determine that he does his best to see only the best in people. His advanced age and years of traveling make him open to other people's differences.

Hamra Ranthas

Townspeople joke that Hamra (female human **veteran**) is a soft-spoken woman with a big axe. Her soft voice is partly due to the large scars traveling down the side of her face and neck. The scars came in a battle with a large troll that invaded nearby forests. Standing well over 6-feet-tall and possessing dark black hair and eyes, she is a rather imposing figure. While she doesn't talk much, most of the townspeople find her presence quite calming.

Hamra and her deputies discovered Londar's overturned carriage and the body of his driver shortly after his disappearance. She is able to tell the characters where the carriage was found and describe the additional bodies that were found there. Four of the thieves or kidnappers that attacked the carriage were clearly killed by fire or electrical spells of some sort, while a fifth appeared to have been killed by Londar's driver. Hamra originally believed that Londar was kidnapped but now suspects Londar somehow escaped. A week after the discovery, she and several village guards accompanied Learah Relight on a foray to the mansion where they found extensive looting. There was no sign of Londar, but "animated statues" and several deadly traps prevented a more thorough investigation. She finds the lack of a body or ransom note disturbing but believes that it is outside her duty to investigate any further because the accident was outside her territory and the search would reduce defenses for Hampton Hill. Furthermore, she believes further exploration of the tower is beyond the abilities of her guards and doesn't want to risk their life. To cut down on the looting, she has made it clear to all the merchants in town that possessing items taken from Londar's mansion would garner time in the dungeon.

While she actually likes **Learah Relight**, there are bad feelings between the two regarding Hamra's refusal to send guards out to search the mansion again. **Alfguir's** claims about Londar owing him money seem valid and not unreasonable based on the credit she has seen merchants and nobles extend to each other in the past. She knows that Baron Kurell is a baron from the northeast and knows nothing about Ander Fierk.

The Deputies: Anya, Ria, Mik, and Dane

As a whole, all the deputies (male and female human **guards**) are dedicated to their work. They are honest, and respected throughout the town. They direct questions about various people in town to **Learah** or **Strybyorn**.

Other Important Figures in Hampton Hill

Baeris Blackoak

Baeris (female half-elf **commoner**) is a thin half-elf with delicate features and light brown hair. She wears elegant blue and green silk shirts to highlight the pale green color of her eyes and usually wears black linen pants. Although her soft, musical voice and polite manner make her seem very unthreatening, she is rumored to have killed several men who threatened one of her daughters during a bar brawl. Baeris is extremely protective of her daughters and does her best to keep them away from adventurers and other seedy characters while directing them toward wealthy merchants and nobles. Baeris knows a great deal about the local politics of the area and has numerous stories about Londar and the firework displays Londar put on for the townspeople. Londar was a regular guest in the restaurant and usually had his guests stay in The White Boar Inn, so Baeris has only favorable comments about him. While Baeris knows that Learah Relight is Londar's niece and that Londar cared for her when her parents died, she knows very little else. Baeris has heard that Alfguir K'Eliek is an honest, trustworthy merchant and says this if asked about him. She briefly met Ander Fierk one evening and didn't like him, so any comments she makes about Ander are tainted by her own feelings and aren't based on any real knowledge of the wizard's background.

Viarik Kite

Viarik (male human **commoner**) is a tall, heavyset man in his early 40s. Long, graying hair and droopy fat cheeks make him seem like a faithful hound. Brightly colored clothing and a loud voice shake that image, while his polite attitude toward his wealthy customers tends to reinforce it. Viarik loves gossip; in the years since his wife died, he has little else to enjoy. He knows a great deal about local politics, rumors, and gossip. Discussions with Viarik receive advantage on Intelligence (Investigation) checks when gathering information about local affairs. Viarik's opinions and commentaries on anyone in town are easy to obtain, but not always very reliable. He avoids saying anything harmful about any potential clients, but merchants and nobles who own their own homes in the area are always fair game. Viarik is a bit of a coward and doesn't talk about ancient ruins, dungeons, or raiding parties because he is afraid it could bring bad luck.

Kyrean Lane

Kyrean (female human **bandit captain**, but with maximum hit points) is a friendly, dark-haired woman that most people find pleasant and easy to deal with. She keeps her dark side well-hidden from those around her; even members of the thieves' guild haven't seen her cold rage. While working in her shop or wandering around town, she wears bright orange or red dresses, only changing into her armor and carrying her bow when she is "working."

Kyrean is the leader of the local thieves' guild but has deferred to Alfguir K'Eliek while he has been in town. Only she and a few members of her guild know Alfguir's true profession and reasons for being here. Kyrean has lost 2 members of her own guild, and 4 members of other guilds were hired to help Alfguir, so she is very hesitant about sending more guild members to Londar's mansion. If asked about Londar, or about Alfguir, she mentions what a fine gentleman Alfguir is and mentions rumors about Alfguir needing someone to help collect some of Londar's debts. Kyrean wisely uses Hampton Hill as a base to study wealthy visitors so they can be robbed later while they are traveling. She tries to keep thefts in and around town to a minimum to avoid frightening wealthy vacationers away.

Alfguir's quest for payment has been putting her, and some of her guild members, at risk of discovery, so she does her best to encourage adventurers to hire on with Alfguir. Any thefts by non-guild members that are carried out in town immediately incur her wrath and planned retaliation.

Mara Lighthand

Mara (female halfling **priest**) weaves flowers into her long, pale brown hair as she braids it in a single plait down her back. Her clothing tends toward pale greens and browns contrasting sharply with her pale lavender eyes. A friendly, open nature and her constant ministering to the town's healing needs have made her a well-respected, openly loved member of the community. Mara met Londar several times and was taken in completely by his charming nature; she, like most villagers, believes something horrible has happened to him. She doesn't believe that Londar would ever default on a debt and has problems believing Alfguir K'Eliek's story. The fact that Londar missed Learah Relight's wedding makes her feel all the more sorry for his young niece. Characters known to be helping Learah find her uncle are given special treatment, free healing, and advice. Mara is very suspicious of Ander Fierk; she noticed him traveling toward Londar's mansion several times over the past weeks and believes he is up to no good. If Mara is not found at the shrine to Arn, she is probably wandering the town helping people or at The White Boar Inn for a good meal and some entertainment.

Khenden Brightsun

While she openly admits that "Brightsun" (**commoner**) is a stage name, she has never given anyone a different name, so she is known throughout town simply as "Bright." Her golden hair, deep blue eyes, and lilting accent suggest she comes from much farther north, but nobody knows for certain. She wears dark blue and purple clothing trimmed in silver while working in the evenings at The White Boar Inn and brighter colors while walking through town during the day. Despite living in Hampton Hill for more than 3 years, she knows far more about the town, and its people, than anyone knows about her. She knows a great deal about local nobles, noble houses, merchants' guilds, and their backgrounds, but doesn't give up such information easily. Her experiences with Londar led her to believe he has a darker nature that he kept hidden from others. She speaks with Learah Relight regularly and thinks highly of her but has a very low opinion of Baron Kurell and is willing to say so. Comments she has overhead lead her to believe Alfguir is somehow involved with the thieves' guild but she doesn't know in what capacity, nor does she easily provide that information for fear of angering the guild.

Xanthaque

At more than 320 years old, Xanthaque (female elf **archmage**) has witnessed events now considered "history." Her studies carry this knowledge back through hundreds of years. Great age has faded her once golden hair to white but the few wrinkles she does have confine themselves to her hands and arms. Still a very attractive woman, many people in Hampton Hill are fond of her quiet personality and unobtrusive nature. Xanthaque has had bad experiences sharing her spellbooks in the past and is unlikely to be convinced to share them again, unless she has great reason to trust the wizard in question. On the other hand, she loves knowledge and is very focused on historical events and ancient books. Given a few days, she can interpret and analyze any ancient texts the characters might come across.

Xanthaque did some work for Londar and has had many discussions with him. She suspects his disappearance might be linked to some ancient texts he recently discovered. Londar was very excited about these texts, but Xanthaque never had the opportunity to examine them. Xanthaque is one of the few people familiar with Londar's quest for power, something she is unlikely to mention because she considers it normal for a "young" wizard. If the characters bring Xanthaque some of Londar's notes and books, she can explain the text dealing with *Horgrim's Pyramid* and informs the characters that the white metallic sphere required to open it is called *The White Eye*. Her studies allow her to tell the characters about the forgotten evil god Horgrim, his worshippers, and their destruction by forces dedicated to Arn, a minor god of the sun. She is able to tell the characters that the only remaining temple to Horgrim is hidden in a hollow mountain known as "Arn's Mountain" after Arn's forces defeated Horgrim's followers. She can give a general location of the mountain, but with Londar's notes and maps she can give the characters more precise directions. Londar's notes and her own texts describe *The White Eye* as having horrible evil powers, abilities that are enhanced magnified if combined with *Horgrim's Pyramid*.

Appendix B: New Monsters

Blood Wight

This creature looks like a tattered and desiccated humanoid about 8 feet covered in fresh blood which seems to ooze and weep from its body. Its clothes hang in rags and are soaked in blood as well. Its hands end in sharpened claws and its eyes display no signs of life.

When a living creature bleeds to death on unholy ground, its corpse sometimes returns to life as a blood wight. Evil priests of Orcus, Jubilex, Lucifer and various other demon princes and devil lords often hold dark rituals where they bleed a living creature to death in order to create a blood wight. Blood wights generally detest living creatures, but if created by a clerical or necromantic ritual, the created blood wight will not harm its creator (unless attacked first). Blood wights are solitary creatures though occasionally more than one of these creatures is encountered (particularly when they have been created by an evil cleric or necromancer).

A blood wight stands 8 to 10 feet tall and weighs 400 to 550 pounds. It appears much as it did in life but its body constantly weeps and oozes blood, even leaving footprints as it moves across the ground. Blood wights that could speak in life retain the knowledge of all languages they knew, but for the most part blood wights do not communicate either with others of their kind or with living creatures (including their creator).

A blood wight enters combat slashing with its claws. Given a chance, it grabs the closest opponent and engulfs it, holding it inside its body until it drowns. Drowned foes are ejected from the blood wight's body into a heap on the ground (the blood wight later devours any creature it kills).

Blood Wight

Large undead, neutral

Armor Class 16 (natural armor)
Hit Points 95 (10d10 + 40)
Speed 30 ft.

STR	DEX	CON	INT	WIS	CHA
20 (+5)	15 (+2)	18 (+4)	13 (+1)	13 (+1)	16 (+3)

Skills Perception +7, Stealth +5
Damage Resistances fire, necrotic; bludgeoning, piercing, and slashing from nonmagical attacks that aren't silvered
Damage Immunities poison
Condition Immunities exhaustion, poisoned
Senses darkvision 60 ft., passive Perception 17
Languages the languages it knew in life
Challenge 8 (3,900 XP)

Magic Weapons. The wight's weapon attacks are magical.
Sunlight Sensitivity. While in sunlight, the wight has disadvantage on attack rolls, as well as on Wisdom (Perception) checks that rely on sight.

Actions

Multiattack. The blood wight makes one Claw attack and one Life Drain attack.
Claws. *Melee Weapon Attack:* +8 to hit, reach 10 ft., one target. *Hit:* 14 (2d8 + 5) slashing damage. If the target is a Medium or smaller creature, it is grappled (escape DC 15). The wight can grapple only one target.
Engulf. The wight engulfs one creature it has grappled, and the grapple ends. While engulfed, the creature is blinded and restrained, it has total cover against attacks and other effects outside the wight, and it takes 27 (6d8) necrotic damage at the start of each of the wight's turns. If the wight takes 30 damage or more on a single turn from a creature inside it, the wight must succeed on a DC 15 Constitution saving throw at the end of that turn or regurgitate all engulfed creatures, which fall prone in a space within 5 feet of the wight. If the wight dies, all engulfed creatures explode out from the corpse, falling prone 15 feet away.
Life Drain. *Melee Weapon Attack:* +8 to hit, reach 5 ft., one creature. *Hit:* 11 (2d6 + 4) necrotic damage. The target must succeed on a DC 15 Constitution saving throw or its hit point maximum is reduced by an amount equal to the damage taken. This reduction lasts until the target finishes a long rest. The target dies if this effect reduces its hit point maximum to 0. A humanoid slain by this attack rises 24 hours later as a zombie under the wight's control, unless the humanoid is restored to life or its body is destroyed. The wight can have no more than twelve zombies under its control at one time.

Byorik

Large giant, chaotic neutral

Armor Class 15 (natural armor)
Hit Points 126 (12d10 + 60)
Speed 30 ft.

STR	DEX	CON	INT	WIS	CHA
18 (+4)	13 (+1)	20 (+5)	12 (+1)	17 (+3)	12 (+1)

Skills Nature +5, Perception +7, Stealth +5
Senses darkvision 60 ft., passive Perception 17
Languages Common, Druidic, Giant
Challenge 9 (5,000 XP)

Keen smell. Byorik has advantage on Wisdom (Perception) checks that rely on scent.
Regeneration. Byorik regains 10 hit points at the start of his turn. If he takes acid or fire damage the trait doesn't function at the start of his next turn. Byorik dies only if he starts his turn with 0 hit points and does not regenerate.
Spellcasting. Byorik is a 4th-level spellcaster and uses Wisdom as his spellcasting ability (spell save DC 15, spell attack +7). He has the following spells prepared:
Cantrips (at will): *mending, resistance, shillelagh*
1st level (4 slots): *charm person, detect magic, entangle, faerie fire, speak with animals*
2nd level (3 slots): *barkskin, hold person, moonbeam, pass without trace*

Actions

Multiattack. Byorik makes one Bite attack and two Claw attacks.
Bite. *Melee Weapon Attack:* +8 to hit, reach 5 ft., 1 target. *Hit:* 7 (1d6 + 4) piercing damage.
Claw. *Melee Weapon Attack:* +8 to hit, reach 5 ft., 1 target. *Hit:* 11 (2d6 + 4) piercing damage.

Celadra

Medium humanoid (human), chaotic neutral

Armor Class 11
Hit Points 18 (4d6 + 4)
Speed 30 ft.

STR	DEX	CON	INT	WIS	CHA
10 (+0)	12 (+1)	12 (+1)	17 (+3)	13 (+1)	8 (-1)

Skills Arcana +5, Stealth +3
Senses passive Perception 11
Languages Common, Draconic
Challenge 4 (1,100 XP)

Spellcasting. Celadra is a 4th-level spellcaster and uses Intelligence as her spellcasting ability (save DC 13, spell attack +5). She can cast the following spells (she has already expended a few spell slots today):
Cantrips (at will): *acid splash, light, mage hand, prestidigitation*
1st level (2 slots): *burning hands, mage armor, magic missile, sleep*
2nd level (1 slot): *scorching ray, web*

Actions

Dagger. *Melee Weapon Attack:* +3 to hit, reach 5 ft., 1 target. *Hit:* 3 (1d4 + 1) piercing damage

Chaos Beast

This creature resembles a lion with dark, blackened fur, razor-sharp fangs, and oversized paws that wield sharpened claws.

A beast of chaos is a creature that has been warped when the demonic forces of the Abyss reach into the Material Plane. A beast of chaos vaguely resembles the animal it once was. Its skin and fur become leprous and patchy. Its color fades to a dull sheen. Its teeth become razor-sharp and more pronounced. Its eyes turn to a bright golden yellow.

Chaos Beast
Medium aberration, chaotic neutral

Armor Class 16 (natural armor)
Hit Points 120 (16d8 + 48)
Speed 30 ft.

STR	DEX	CON	INT	WIS	CHA
17 (+3)	15 (+2)	16 (+3)	10 (+0)	12 (+1)	7 (–2)

Skills Perception +7
Damage Resistances acid, necrotic, slashing
Condition Immunities blinded, charmed, deafened, exhaustion, frightened, prone
Senses darkvision 60 ft., passive Perception 17
Languages None
Challenge 6 (2,300 XP)

Amorphous. The chaos beast can move through a space as narrow as 1 inch wide without squeezing.

Destabilize. A creature that touches the chaos beast or hits it with a melee attack while within 5 feet of it must make a DC 15 Constitution saving throw or be poisoned for 1 minute. A creature poisoned in this way takes 21 (6d6) necrotic damage at the start of each of its turns. It can repeat the saving throw at the end of each of its turns, ending the effect on itself on a success. If the creature's saving throw is successful or the effect ends for it, the creature is immune to the chaos beast's Destabilize for the next 24 hours.

Actions

Multiattack. The chaos beast makes two claw attacks.

Claws. *Melee Weapon Attack:* +6 to hit, reach 5 ft., one target. *Hit:* 10 (2d6 + 3) slashing damage plus 10 (3d6) necrotic damage. The creature must make a DC 15 Constitution saving throw or be affected by the chaos beast's Destabilize effect.

Chrystone

Chrystones are creatures made of rock and crystal that normally stand just over 5 feet tall. Their coloration varies by the types of crystal and rock they absorb, and which give each chrystone a unique pattern of striations and coloration that makes it easy to tell them apart. Chrystone are generally humanoid in shape, with a few small differences. They have almost no neck; their heads seem attached firmly to their shoulders but are still able to turn freely. Each of their hands has two fingers and two opposable thumbs that make their grip quite strong. Originally imbued with life by Londar Brightrain in a ritual involving the blood of several dragons and a demon, chrystones grow new offspring through budding. To form a new bud, a chrystone must consume several times its weight in crystals and consume at least 300 gp worth of gems. The bud continues to grow from the chrystone's back until it is large enough to separate. Each chrystone offspring retains the memories and knowledge of its entire parental line.

Chrystone were originally created to be part of an army but those plans were cut short by their creator's death. As they developed and spread, they became more free-willed and independent and wish to make certain they are never enslaved again. They retain all the abilities that would have made them a powerful army, and their racial knowledge helps them put these abilities to the best possible use. Chrystones, while usually neutral, have a racial memory of being slaves to the whim of their creator. This memory makes them somewhat paranoid when dealing with other races and makes them more likely to attack other races than talk with them.

Combat

Chrystone open with their breath weapon attack and close for melee combat if targets are close enough; otherwise, they stand back and fight with their longswords. If a battle is going poorly, a chrystone attempts to retreat and ambush its opponents when it has repaired itself.

Chrystone
Medium construct, unaligned

Armor Class 15 (natural)
Hit Points 45 (7d8 + 14)
Speed 20 ft.

STR	DEX	CON	INT	WIS	CHA
15 (+2)	9 (–1)	14 (+ 2)	8 (–1)	11 (+0)	1 (–5)

Condition Immunities charmed, exhaustion, fatigued, paralyzed, petrified, poisoned
Damage Resistance bludgeoning, slashing, and piercing damage from nonmagical weapons
Damage Vulnerabilities thunder
Senses darkvision 60 ft, passive Perception 10
Languages common
Challenge 4 (1,100 XP)

Death shatter. When a chrystone dies, it shatters and inflicts 7 (2d6) slashing damage to all creatures within 5 feet (a successful DC 13 Dexterity saving throw for half damage). A chrystone may prevent itself from shattering with a successful DC 15 Wisdom saving throw, though most don't bother.

Immutable form. Chrystones are immune to any effect that would alter their form.

Magic resistance. Chrystones have advantage on all saving throws against magical effects.

Stone shape. Chrystone can use the *stoneshape* spell at will, with Wisdom as their spellcasting ability. They can also use this as an action to heal 1d6 hit points or to create new weapons.

Actions

Longsword. *Melee Weapon Attack:* +4 to hit, reach 5 ft., one target, *Hit:* 6 (1d8 + 2) slashing damage.

Rainbow breath (recharge 5–6). The chrystone breathes a 25-foot cone of rainbow colors that is the equivalent of a *color spray* spell (save DC 12).

Copper Statue

Created much in the same manner as golems, copper statues are multi-limbed, insect-like guardians. These constructs are often used by temples to protect treasuries, holy sites, and other important locales. They are much more reliable than flesh golems and have the added bonus of adhering closer to many faiths' restrictions on the use of living flesh in magical works. They are also cheaper and easier to make than iron golems, while at the same time providing that certain luster that only a metal golem can.

Copper Statue
Large construct, unaligned

Armor Class 18 (natural armor)
Hit Points 90 (12d10 + 24)
Speed 40 ft.

STR	DEX	CON	INT	WIS	CHA
19 (+4)	18 (+4)	15 (+2)	6 (−2)	15 (+2)	7 (−2)

Skills Perception +6
Damage Vulnerabilities. Cold, fire
Damage Resistances. Thunder, and also bludgeoning, piercing, and slashing damage from nonmagical weapons
Damage Immunities. Psychic, poison, and lightning
Condition Immunities. Charmed, exhaustion, fatigued, paralyzed, petrified, and poisoned
Senses darkvision, blindsight 60 ft. passive Perception 16
Languages Can't speak but understands the language of its creator
Challenge 9 (5,000 XP)

Electrically charged. When the copper statue suffers lightning damage, its lightning arc attack is recharged, and the construct gains the effects of a *haste* spell until the end of its next turn. When the construct suffers cold or fire damage, it suffers the effects of a *slow* spell until the end of its next turn. Being under the effects of a *haste* and *slow* spell cancel each other out.
Immutable form. The copper statue is immune to any spell or effect that would alter its form.
Magical weapons. The copper statue's attacks are considered magical weapons

Actions

Multiattack. The copper statue can make two Smash attacks, or one Smash attack and one Lightning Arc.
Slash. *Melee Weapon Attack:* +8 to hit, reach 10 ft., one target. *Hit:* 13 (2d8 + 4) slashing damage.
Lightning arc (recharge 5–6). *Ranged Weapon Attack:* +8 to hit, range 20/120 ft., 1–3 targets. *Hit:* 23 (3d12 + 4) lightning damage.

Dark Warden

Only Horgrim's most faithful followers survive the complex ritual required to become a dark warden. Each dark warden willing gives up its soul, using the energy derived from its consumption and destruction to obtain special, frightening characteristics. The requirements are stringent, and few survive the complex ritual, which burns off all body hair the person might have possessed and turns their skin a deep green or black color. Although usually used as guards for temples and treasuries, it is interesting to note that dark wardens, unlike some undead, do not suffer any damage or loss of ability in sunlight. Although among the most powerful undead, the ritual used to create them burns away the personality and desires of the base creature, leaving behind only the raw intelligence, wisdom, and skills they possessed before the ritual. Dark wardens gain a tireless devotion to their duties at the same time as they lose all desire for personal gain, glory, or further knowledge. This makes them unparalleled, tireless guardians, but also makes the process unattractive to those that seek to "live" beyond their time. Most dark wardens were once monks, warriors, or assassins dedicated to Horgrim's service, but many other faithful followers sacrificed their souls to serve Horgrim for eternity.

Dark Warden
Medium undead, lawful evil

Armor Class 20 (plate armor and shield)
Hit Points 130 (20d8 + 40)
Speed 30 ft.

STR	DEX	CON	INT	WIS	CHA
20 (+5)	19 (+4)	15 (+2)	14 (+2)	10 (+0)	14 (+2)

Skills Perception +4
Condition Immunities charmed, exhaustion, frightened, paralyzed, poisoned
Damage Immunities poison damage
Damage Resistances cold, fire, and thunder, as well as bludgeoning, piercing, and slashing damage from nonmagical weapons
Senses darkvision 60 ft., passive Perception 14
Languages —
Challenge 9 (5,000 XP)

Innate Spellcasting. The dark warden's innate spellcasting ability is Charisma (spell save DC 14). It can innately cast the following spells, requiring no spell components:
(at-will): *bane, haste, enhance ability*
(1/day): *bestow curse*
Turn resistance. The dark warden has advantage on saving throws to resist any effect that turns undead.

Actions

Multiattack. The dark warden makes two Spear attacks or a Spear attack and a Scream.
Scream. The dark warden lets loose a horrid scream. All creatures within 30 feet of the dark warden must succeed at a DC 14 Constitution saving throw or suffer 14 (3d8) thunder damage and gain the deafened condition until the end of their next turn (half damage on a successful save and not deafened).
Spear. *Melee Weapon Attack:* +9 to hit, reach 5 ft., one creature, *Hit:* 9 (1d8 + 5) piercing and 4 (1d8) necrotic.

Dourala
Medium humanoid (human), lawful evil

Armor Class 18 (plate armor)
Hit Points 77 (9d10 + 27)
Speed 30 ft.

STR	DEX	CON	INT	WIS	CHA
19 (+4)	10 (+0)	16 (+3)	11 (+0)	12 (+1)	13 (+1)

Senses passive Perception 11
Languages Common, Infernal
Challenge 9 (5,000 XP)

Action surge. Dourala may take an extra action and may do so twice before taking a long rest.
Heavy weapon mastery. Dourala rerolls 1s and 2s on damage dice when using a two-handed weapon.
Second Wind. As a bonus action, Dourala recovers 1d10 + 9 hit points.

Actions

Multiattack. Dourala makes two Greatsword attacks.
Greatsword. *Melee Weapon Attack:* +8 to hit, reach 5 ft., 1 target. *Hit:* 11 (2d6 + 4) slashing damage.

Dragon Statue

These rare constructs are made from the bones and scales of a slain adult or larger dragon. Animated by the same type of magic that creates golems, dragon statues are more of a thematic addition to any mad wizard's tower than a replacement for a more common golem. Calling upon the power and fury of the dragon, dragon statues vary according to the dragon whose body parts are used to make them.

Dragon Statue

Large construct, unaligned

Armor Class 14 (natural armor)
Hit Points 165 (22d10 + 44)
Speed 40 ft.

STR	DEX	CON	INT	WIS	CHA
20 (+5)	14 (+2)	14 (+2)	7 (−2)	7 (−2)	11 (+0)

Damage Vulnerabilities Varies by color
Damage Immunities Varies by color, as well as psychic and poison
Damage Resistances Bludgeoning, piercing, and slashing from nonmagical attacks
Condition Immunities Charmed, exhaustion, fatigued, paralyzed, petrified, and poisoned
Senses darkvision 60 ft; passive Perception 8
Languages Can't speak but understand the language of its creator
Challenge 10 (5,900 XP)

Immutable form. The dragon statue is immune to any spell or effect that would alter its form.
Magical weapons. The dragon statue's attacks are considered magical.

Actions

Multiattack. The dragon statue makes two melee attacks.
Bite. *Melee Weapon Attack:* +9 to hit, reach 10 ft., one target. *Hit:* 14 (2d8 + 5) piercing damage.
Claw. *Melee Weapon Attack:* +9 to hit, reach 5 ft., one target. *Hit:* 14 (2d8 + 5) slashing damage.
Breath weapon (recharge 5–6). The dragon statue breathes out a 40-foot cone of energy (as determined by the type of dragon it was made from). Any creature caught in the cone must make a DC 16 Dexterity saving throw or suffer 21 (6d6) damage of a type determined by the dragon from which the statue was made, as well as suffering the associated condition until the end of its next turn (half damage and no condition on successful save)

Dragon Statue Vulnerabilities, Immunities, and Energy Damage

Color	Vulnerability	Immunity	Breath Weapon	Condition
Black	Radiant	Poison	Poison	Poisoned
Blue	Cold	Lightning	Lightning	Stunned
Brass	Cold	Fire	Fire	Blinded
Bronze	Cold	Lightning	Lightning	Stunned
Copper	Cold	Acid	Acid	Blinded
Green	Cold	Poison	Poison	Poisoned
Gold	Cold	Fire	Fire	Blinded
Red	Cold	Fire	Fire	Blinded
Silver	Fire	Cold	Cold	Paralyzed
White	Fire	Cold	Cold	Paralyzed

Fungus Gargoyle

This creature looks like a winged statue, humanoid in shape, carved from molds, funguses, and mushrooms. Its arms and legs end in clawed hands and feet, and its mouth is lined with fangs carved from the same substances its body is.

Fungus gargoyles are thought to be gargoyles that have been transformed into their current state by an evil cult that pays reverence to various demons of slime, ooze, and fungus. These creatures are often found acting as guardians in temples dedicated to such demons.

Unlike normal plants, fungus gargoyles do not require food or air (they still require water, however), but sometimes eat their fallen enemies simply for the sheer pleasure of doing so (usually only evil-aligned fungus gargoyles do this). A typical fungus gargoyle stands about 5 or 6 feet tall and weighs up to 200 pounds. Though its shape can vary, most resemble ugly winged humanoids.

Fungus gargoyles typically ambush their prey, standing motionless until their opponent moves close. The fungus gargoyles then leap to the attack, slashing with their claws. Most fungus gargoyles try to stay airborne during combat rather than fight on the ground.

Fungus Gargoyle

Medium plant, neutral evil

Armor Class 14 (natural armor)
Hit Points 67 (9d8 + 27)
Speed 30 ft., fly 60 ft.

STR	DEX	CON	INT	WIS	CHA
18 (+4)	14 (+2)	17 (+3)	6 (−2)	11 (+0)	7 (−2)

Skills Perception +6, Stealth +5
Damage Resistances fire; bludgeoning, piercing, and slashing from nonmagical weapons that aren't adamantine
Damage Immunities poison
Condition Immunities exhaustion, petrified, poisoned
Senses passive Perception 16
Languages —
Challenge 5 (1,800 XP)

False Appearance. While the gargoyle remains motionless, it is indistinguishable from a weathered, inanimate statue that is covered in fungus, lichen, and moss.
Stench. Any creature that starts its turn within 10 feet of the gargoyle must succeed on a DC 13 Constitution saving throw or be poisoned until the start of its next turn. On a successful saving throw, the creature is immune to the gargoyle's stench for 24 hours.

Actions

Multiattack. The gargoyle makes three attacks: one with its bite and two with its claws.
Bite. *Melee Weapon Attack:* +7 to hit, reach 5 ft., one target. *Hit:* 13 (2d8 + 4) piercing damage.
Claws. *Melee Weapon Attack:* +7 to hit, reach 5 ft., one target. *Hit:* 11 (2d6 + 4) slashing damage.
Deadly Spores (recharge 5–6). The fungus gargoyle exhales deadly spores in a 15-foot cone. Each creature in the area must make a DC 15 Constitution saving throw, taking 18 (4d8) poison damage on a failed save, or half as much damage on a successful one.

Ice Elemental

Coldly dispassionate, these rare elementals hail from the cooler parts of the Elemental Plane of Water. Disliked by other water elementals due to their rigid thoughts and poor disposition, ice elementals in turn hate their brethren. Ice elementals have bodies made of solid ice often veined with streaks of pale blue. In the right light they are nearly invisible until the move, nothing showing but their dark blue eyespots. Rarely seen outside of their home place, sometimes one can find ice elementals in the coldest places of the world. Also, mad wizards are known to summon and bind them for esoteric purposes, not the least of which is making strange sculpture gardens.

Greater Pyrohydra

Huge monstrosity, unaligned

Armor Class 17 (natural armor)
Hit Points 218 (19d12 + 95)
Speed 30 ft., swim 30 ft.

STR	DEX	CON	INT	WIS	CHA
21 (+5)	12 (+1)	21 (+5)	2 (–4)	10 (+0)	7 (–2)

Skills Perception +10
Damage Immunities fire
Senses darkvision 60 ft., passive Perception 20
Languages —
Challenge 16 (15,000 XP)

Hold Breath. The greater pyrohydra can hold its breath for one hour.
Multiple Heads. The greater pyrohydra has nine heads. While it has more than one head, the greater pyrohydra has advantage on saving throws against being blinded, charmed, deafened, frightened, stunned, and knocked unconscious.

Whenever the greater pyrohydra takes 25 or more damage in a single turn, one of its heads dies. If all its heads die, the greater pyrohydra dies.

At the end of its turn, it grows two heads (up to a maximum of eighteen heads) for each of its heads that died since its last turn, unless it has taken acid or cold damage since its last turn. The greater pyrohydra regains 10 hit points for each head regrown in this way.

If the pyophydra has more than nine heads, it loses one of its heads when it takes a long rest.

Reactive Heads. For each head the elder pyrohydra has beyond one, it gets an extra reaction that can be used only for opportunity attacks.
Wakeful. While the greater pyrohydra sleeps, at least one of its heads is awake.

Actions

Multiattack. The greater pyrohydra makes one Bite attack with each head.
Bite. *Melee Weapon Attack*: +10 to hit, reach 10 ft., one target. *Hit*: 10 (1d10 + 5) piercing damage plus 5 (2d4) cold damage.
Fire Breath (recharge 5–6). The greater pyrohydra uses all its heads to exhale flame which fills a 25-foot radius sphere centered on a point it chooses within 50 feet of it. Each creature in that area must make a DC 18 Dexterity saving throw, taking 63 (18d6) fire damage on a failed save or half as much on a successful one.

Ice Elemental

Huge elemental, Neutral

Armor Class 16 (natural armor)
Hit Points 114 (12d10 + 48)
Speed 20 ft.

STR	DEX	CON	INT	WIS	CHA
18 (+4)	14 (+2)	18 (+4)	5 (-3)	10 (+0)	6 (–3)

Damage Vulnerabilities Fire
Damage Resistances Acid, bludgeoning, piercing, and slashing damage from nonmagical attacks
Damage Immunities Cold
Condition Immunities Exhaustion, paralyzed, petrified, poisoned, unconscious
Senses darkvision 60 ft., passive Perception 10
Languages aquan
Challenge 9 (5,000 XP)

Creature of cold. When the ice elemental would suffer cold damage, it regains half the damage as HP and its breath weapon recharges.
Made of ice. Ice elementals float in liquid.

Actions

Multiattack. The ice elemental makes two Smash attacks.
Slam. *Melee Weapon Attack:* +8 to hit, reach 10 ft., one target. *Hit:* 13 (2d8 + 4) bludgeoning and 9 (2d8) cold damage
Cold Breath (recharge 5–6). The ice elemental breathes out a 15-foot cone of freezing cold. All creatures caught in the cone must succeed at a DC 16 Constitution saving throw or suffer 18 (4d8) cold damage and be stunned until the end of their next turn (half damage and not stunned on a successful save)

Lead Skeleton

This creature appears to be an animated skeleton whose bones have been coated with metal.

Lead skeletons appear simply to be skeletons coated with metal. Despite their outward appearance, they are actually golem-like constructs and not undead. Therefore, they cannot be turned.

Lead skeletons appear as 6-foot-tall skeletons constructed of metal. Some have gemstones encrusted in the body and eye sockets. A lead skeleton is expensive to create. Those who choose to create such creatures prefer the added fear and awe the skeletons tend to receive, and have a great deal of additional wealth and time.

Lead skeletons can be programmed to attack only certain creatures or be programmed to accept certain passwords or types of clothing. More complex programming tends to fail. While lead skeletons might not have the same abilities as other golems, their immunities and speed make them extraordinarily dangerous. They use their fists to inflict large amounts of damage and attack a single target until it is dead.

Lead Skeleton

Medium undead, neutral

Armor Class 18 (natural armor)
Hit Points 66 (12d8 + 12)
Speed 30 ft.

STR	DEX	CON	INT	WIS	CHA
21 (+5)	18 (+4)	13 (+1)	2 (–4)	10 (+0)	1 (–5)

Damage Immunities acid, cold, fire, lightning, poison; bludgeoning, piercing, and slashing from nonmagical attacks that aren't adamantine
Condition Immunities charmed, exhaustion, frightened, paralyzed, petrified, poisoned
Senses darkvision 60 ft., passive Perception 10
Languages understands the languages it knew in life but can't speak
Challenge 6 (2,300 XP)

Immutable Form. The skeleton is immune to any spell or effect that would alter its form.
Magic Resistance. The skeleton has advantage on saving throws against spells and other magical effects.
Magic Weapons. The skeleton's weapon attacks are magical.

Actions

Multiattack. The lead skeleton makes two Slam attacks.
Slams. *Melee Weapon Attack:* +8 to hit, reach 5 ft., one target. *Hit:* 14 (2d8 + 5) bludgeoning damage.

Lich Shade

This creature appears as a rotting and skeletal humanoid dressed in tattered and worn robes with ancient runes etched on their surface. Its eyes blaze with a crimson fire.

The road a spellcaster travels in his or her quest for lichdom is not without danger. During the dark rituals invoked to achieve lichdom, the caster sometimes errs in his or her calculations or unleashes mystic forces best left untapped. When such an event occurs, the spellcaster is usually destroyed outright. Other times, something is born as a result of this failed ritual — a lich shade.

Lich shades are evil creatures who attempted to achieve lichdom but failed for whatever reason. The creature is not destroyed, nor does it become a lich, it becomes something in between — something in between mortal life and eternal unlife.

Lich shades retain portions of their life's memories and always retain full memory of the dark ritual they attempted while trying to become a lich. For this reason alone, they have grown to hate the living and particularly living spellcasters whom they blame (in some warp twisted way) for their current condition. A lich shade always attacks any opponents who have a spellcaster in their midst, often targeting that individual directly above all others.

A lich shade stands about 6 to 6-1/2 feet tall and weighs about 160 pounds. The robes and gowns it wears often denote its previous life's profession (wizardly robes or priestly vestments for example).

A lich shade attacks with its powerful claws, rending and tearing at its foes. If facing a spellcaster and it leeches one of its spells, it usually releases the first spell leeched as an eldritch bolt against its closest foe. Further leeched spells are used to heal the lich shade or cast back against its foes. If faced with certain defeat, a lich shade wills its own destruction, invoking its death throes ability, hoping to take several of its opponents with it.

A lich shade's natural weapons are treated as magic weapons for the purpose of overcoming damage reduction.

Lich Shade

Medium undead, neutral evil

Armor Class 16 (natural armor)
Hit Points 85 (9d8 + 45)
Speed 30 ft.

STR	DEX	CON	INT	WIS	CHA
11 (+0)	16 (+3)	20 (+5)	18 (+4)	16 (+3)	13 (+1)

Skills Arcana +7, History +7, Insight +6, Perception +6
Damage Resistances cold, lightning, poison; bludgeoning, piercing, and slashing damage from nonmagical attacks
Damage Immunities necrotic
Condition Immunities charmed, exhaustion, frightened, paralyzed, poisoned
Senses darkvision 60 ft., passive Perception 16
Languages Common, Infernal, plus up to four other languages
Challenge 8 (3,900 XP)

Death Throes. When the lich shade drops to 0 hit points, it explodes in a cloud of dust in a 10-foot radius. Creatures within this area must make a DC 16 Constitution saving throw. On a failed saving throw, the creature takes 22 (4d10) necrotic damage, and the creature's maximum hit points are reduced by the same amount. If a creature's maximum hit points are reduced to 0, it dies. Magic such as *greater restoration* is necessary to cure this effect. On a successful saving throw, the creature takes half damage and is poisoned for 1 minute, but its maximum hit points are unaffected.
Magic Resistance. The lich shade has advantage on saving throws against spells and other magical effects.
Magic Weapon. The lich shade's weapon attacks are magical.

Actions

Multiattack. The lich shade makes two claw attacks.
Claw. *Melee Weapon Attack:* +6 to hit, reach 5 ft., one target. *Hit:* 12 (2d8 + 3) slashing damage plus 11 (2d10) cold damage.

Reactions

Spell Leech. When a creature the lich shade can see within 30 feet of it casts a spell of 1st level or higher, the lich shade can counter the spell, as if the lich shade had cast *counterspell*. If the lich shade attempts to leech a spell of 4th level or higher, it must make an Intelligence ability check. The DC for this check is 10 + the spell's level.
If the spell leech is successful, the lich shade absorbs the magical energy and can use it only on its next turn in one of the following ways:
Cast. The lich shade can cast the spell as an action on its turn, using the original caster's spell save DC and spell attack modifier.
Eldritch Bolt. The lich shade chooses one creature it can see within 60 feet of it as an action. That creature must make a DC 16 Dexterity saving throw, taking 22 (4d10) force damage on a failed saving throw, or half as much damage on a successful one.
Heal. The lich shade uses an action to regain 22 (4d10) hit points, up to its maximum hit points.
If the lich shade does not use the absorbed magic, it fades at the end of its next turn.

Golem, Magnesium

Silvery-white powder shakes loose from this construct as it stomps across the floor. Its face is a featureless plane except for two gouges where there should be eyes.

Magnesium golems are silvery-white humanoids created by arcane spellcasters. As with other golems, they are incapable of thinking on their own, and are thus under control of the one that created them. They are created as guardians and keepers and can be given specific orders to guard a specific locale, item, or object or to attack a specific creature or type of creature.

The magnesium golem is a silvery-white humanoid formed of magnesium. The average magnesium golem stands about 6–7 feet tall and weighs 600 pounds. The magnesium golem's features are smooth and perfect, though it has no discernable ears, nose, or mouth. Its eyes appear to be nothing more than indentations in its body. Magnesium golems wear no clothing and never carry weapons, and it cannot speak or make any vocal noise. Unlike many other golems, the magnesium golem can move at the same speed as a human of its size.

Magnesium Golem

Medium construct, neutral

Armor Class 15 (natural armor)
Hit Points 68 (8d8 + 32)
Speed 30 ft.

STR	DEX	CON	INT	WIS	CHA
19 (+4)	9 (–1)	18 (+4)	6 (–2)	10 (+0)	5 (–3)

Damage Immunities fire, poison, psychic; bludgeoning, piercing, and slashing from nonmagical weapons that aren't adamantine
Condition Immunities charmed, exhaustion, frightened, paralyzed, petrified, poisoned
Senses darkvision 60 ft., passive Perception 10
Languages understands the languages of its creator but can't speak
Challenge 5 (1,800 XP)

Aura of Sickness. Creatures who begin their turn within 10 feet of the golem must make a DC 15 Constitution saving throw. On a failed saving throw, the creature is poisoned for 1 minute. If a creature ends its turn outside the 10-foot area, it can repeat the saving throw, ending the effect on a success. If the creature succeeds or if the effect ends for it, it is immune to the golem's aura of sickness for 24 hours.
Fire Absorption. Whenever the golem is subjected to fire damage, it takes no damage and instead regains a number of hit points equal to the fire damage dealt.
Immutable Form. The golem is immune to any spell or effect that would alter its form.
Magic Resistance. The golem has advantage on saving throws against spells and other magical effects.
Magic Weapon. The golem's weapon attacks are magical.

Actions

Multiattack. The golem makes two slam attacks.
Slam. *Melee Weapon Attack:* +7 to hit, reach 5 ft., one target. *Hit:* 13 (2d8 + 4) bludgeoning damage.

Murder Creeper

Found in the jungles of the world, the murder creeper is a carnivorous plant that can uproot itself to find better nutrients. Usually, the murder creeper is happy to stay put and send out long tendrils to grasp prey and draw it in. After the life of the unfortunate animal is squeezed out, the carcass is left to decay and thus feed the creeper's roots. When prey is scarce, the murder creeper pulls itself up by its roots and drags itself around the jungle in search of a suitable place to root. If no decaying carcass of suitable size is found, the murder creeper is not above lying in ambush and making one.

Murder Creeper

Medium plant, unaligned

Armor Class 15 (natural armor)
Hit Points 39 (6d8 + 12)
Speed 10 ft.

STR	DEX	CON	INT	WIS	CHA
14 (+2)	10 (+0)	15 (+2)	3 (–4)	12 (+1)	3 (–4)

Skills Perception +3, Stealth +2
Damage Vulnerabilities fire
Damage Resistances Bludgeoning and piercing
Senses low-light vision; passive Perception 13
Languages none
Challenge 3 (700 XP)

Jungle Creature. The murder creeper has advantage on Dexterity (Stealth) checks in forests, jungles, grasslands, and other natural environments.
Blood Drain. If the murder creeper hits a target with its tendril attack, the target must succeed at a DC 12 Constitution saving throw or lose a hit die.

Actions

Multiattack. The murder creeper makes two Tendril attacks.
Tendrils. *Melee Weapon Attack:* +4 to hit, reach 10 ft., one target. *Hit:* 6 (1d8 + 2) piercing damage

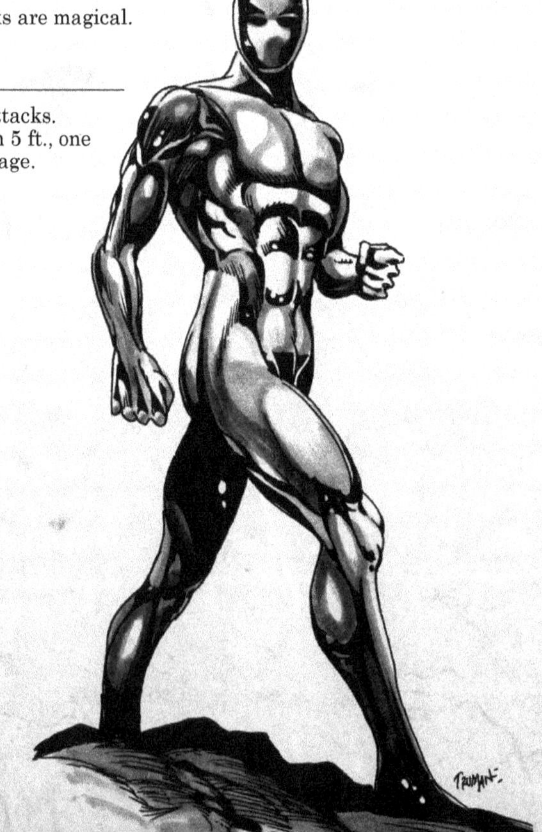

Tiger Lord

Even the wisest of sages have no idea where the animal lords come from. Some say they are the scions of a union between angels and animals, while others claim to have proof that the gods of forests and jungles created the animal lords to oversee their creation. A rare few, though they might be on the right track, say that the animal lords are just really old animals. According to this theory, certain animals simply do not die but just keep getting larger, more intelligent, and more fearsome until they become to the lesser members of their species as kings are to peasants.

Tiger lords are mighty tigers who are the paragons of what it means to be a tiger. They are much larger than common tigers, more intelligent, blessed with the gift of speech, and possessing of terrible powers that border on magic. Perfect specimens of tigerness, tiger lords have sleek fur over muscled bodies, sharp fangs larger than swords, and claws that would give a wyvern pause or even envy.

Tiger Lord

Huge magical beast, neutral

Armor Class 17 (natural armor)
Hit Points 143 (15d12 + 45)
Speed 40 ft., climb 30 ft.

STR	DEX	CON	INT	WIS	CHA
22 (+6)	20 (+5)	17 (+3)	13 (+1)	17 (+3)	14 (+2)

Skills Perception +6
Damage Resistances Bludgeoning, piercing, and slashing damage from nonmagical weapons
Senses low-light vision, darkvision 60 ft., passive Perception 16
Languages Celestial, Common
Challenge 8 (3,900 XP)

Lord of Tigers. The tiger lord is master of all tigers. When it uses its roar action, any tigers within 1 mile rush to obey the tiger lord, fighting to the death for it.
Rend. If a creature is struck by two claw attacks using the multiattack action, it suffers an additional 9 (2d8) slashing damage.

Actions

Multiattack. The tiger lord makes two melee attack.
Bite. *Melee Weapon Attack:* +9 to hit, reach 5 ft., one target. *Hit:* 24 (4d8 + 6) piercing damage.
Claw. *Melee Weapon Attack:* +9 to hit, reach 10 ft., one target. *Hit:* 15 (2d8 + 6) slashing damage.
Roar (recharge 5–6). The tiger lord lets loose a mighty roar that shakes the trees and splits the rocks. This roar can be heard for miles, but up close it is powerful enough to shred flesh and tear metal. All creatures in a 40-foot cone centered on the tiger must succeed at a DC 14 Constitution saving throw or suffer 18 (4d8) thunder damage and gain the frightened condition until the end of their next turn (half damage on a successful save and not frightened).

Violet and Krybern

Medium humanoid (human), neutral evil

Armor Class 15 (studded leather)
Hit Points 22 (4d8 + 4)
Speed 30 ft.

STR	DEX	CON	INT	WIS	CHA
10 (+0)	17 (+3)	12 (+1)	12 (+1)	10 (+0)	14 (+2)

Skills Perception +2, Stealth +7, Thieves' tools +7
Senses passive Perception 12
Languages Common, Elven, Halfling
Challenge 4 (1,100 XP)

Evasion. If subject to an effect that would allow them to make a Dexterity saving throw for half damage, these two rascals instead suffer no damage from the attack on a successful save, and half damage if they fail.
Sneak attack. If either of these two rascals gain advantage on an attack roll or they have an ally within 5 feet of a target, they inflict an additional 2d6 damage with a successful attack.

Actions

Shortsword. *Melee Weapon Attack:* +5 to hit, reach 5 ft., 1 target. *Hit:* 6 (1d6 + 3) piercing damage.
Light crossbow. *Ranged Weapon Attack:* +5 to hit, range (80/320), 1 target. *Hit:* 7 (1d8 + 3) piercing damage

Wood Golem

This automaton is human-sized and resembles an ornately carved wooden statue.

Arcane spellcasters used several ancient texts to arrive at a process to create inexpensive yet still quite powerful golems. They had master craftsmen create wood statues with articulating limbs and then performed the proper spells to animate and control them. The statues vary in shape and form and usually have weapons of some sort held in each hand. The wood golems were designed to act both as an alarm and a protection against intruders.

Wood golems are usually programmed to close doors and avoid ranged weapons and spells but do not break off melee combat to avoid missile fire from other sources. They attack with their fists.

Wood Golem

Medium construct, neutral

Armor Class 13 (natural armor)
Hit Points 45 (7d8 + 14)
Speed 30 ft.

STR	DEX	CON	INT	WIS	CHA
16 (+3)	10 (+0)	15 (+2)	7 (–2)	11 (+0)	5 (–3)

Damage Vulnerabilities fire
Damage Immunities cold, lightning, poison, psychic; bludgeoning, piercing, and slashing damage from nonmagical attacks
Condition Immunities charmed, exhaustion, frightened, paralyzed, petrified, poisoned
Senses darkvision 60 ft., passive Perception 10
Languages understands the languages of its creator but can't speak
Challenge 3 (700 XP)

Alarm. Whenever a creature other than its creator comes within 60 feet of the golem, it releases an audible alarm sound which can be heard out to a range of 300 feet.
Immutable Form. The golem is immune to any spell or effect that would alter its form.
Magic Resistance. The golem has advantage on saving throws against spells and other magical effects.
Magic Weapon. The golem's weapon attacks are magical.

Appendix C: New Cleric

Undeath

The undeath domain, most notably linked to the demonic god Orcus, is used by foul cultists and clerics. It centers around two factors: dying and returning from death as an abominable perversion of life and goodness. The gods of undeath promote illness, sickness, injury, and any other thing that leads to natural death and the unnatural transformation into undeath. Those that follow these gods tend to be either ambitious reapers of the slain or hopeful types who see eternity as an undead creature preferable to the vicissitudes of life.

Undeath Domain Spells

Cleric Level	Spells
1st	bane, inflict wounds
3rd	darkness, moonbeam
5th	animate dead, speak with dead
7th	fear, vampiric touch
9th	contact outer plane, contagion

Disciple of Undeath

When you choose this domain at 1st level, you gain resistance to necrotic damage.

Channel Divinity: Command Undead

Starting at 2nd level, you can use your Channel Divinity to take control of lesser undead. This effects only undead with an Intelligence score of 6 or less. Any such undead creature that can see you and is within 30 feet must make a Wisdom saving throw. Creatures under the command of another, such as through use of this Channel Divinity or the *animate dead* spell make this save using their controller's saving throw. If the creature fails its save, it gains the charmed condition for a number of hours equal to your Wisdom modifier. Furthermore, you can give the undead an order, such as telling it to attack a creature, step aside, or bring you a drink. When you do so, it may attempt another save, and if successful, the charmed condition ends.

Improved animate dead

Beginning at 6th level, when you cast the *animate dead* spell, you create one additional undead creature.

Divine Strike

At 8th level, you gain the ability to infuse your attacks with necrotic energy. Once on each of your turns when you hit a creature with a weapon attack, you may cause the attack to deal an extra 1d8 necrotic damage to the target. At 14th level, the extra damage increases to 2d8.

Improved Control Undead

At 17th level there is no limit to the intelligence of undead creatures you may attempt to control. Undead creatures with an Intelligence score of 6 or less that you take control of through your Channel Divinity: Control Undead class feature remain under your control.

Appendix D: New Magic Items

Amulet of the Dark Sun

Wondrous item, uncommon (requires attunement by a worshipper of Horgrim)

A symbol of those devoted to Horgrim, an ancient evil god of war and magic, these powerful amulets were used to identify the true faithful and often saw use as keys for some temples. Although the process used to create these relics is now lost, they possess enough power that evil wizards and clerics are willing to pay a high price for any functioning amulets due to the bonuses they give mindless undead. The amulets are made of a mysterious dark metal and engraved with symbols representing Horgrim. Raised markings and designs in gold highlight the engraved symbols and focus attention on them. Made in large batches when Horgrim's worshippers were powerful, most of them were lost and destroyed over the past few thousand years. Designed to weed out traitors and enforce loyalty, the evil power contained by one of these amulets varies depending upon who is wearing one. The evil aura is powerful enough to inflict 7 (2d6) necrotic damage per round to any good-aligned character wearing one and 2 (1d4) necrotic damage per round to any neutral-aligned character. Evil-aligned characters wearing an amulet suffer no penalties or damage, nor do they obtain any bonuses unless they swear fealty to Horgrim while wearing the amulet. Living evil creatures that swear allegiance to Horgrim have permanent *darkvision* while wearing the amulet and can cast *darkness* once per day. Mindless or free-willed undead that swear fealty to Horgrim gain advantage on saving throws against turn undead effects while wearing an amulet and evil fey, fiends, and celestials that pledge themselves to Horgrim gain advantage on saving throws to resist the *banishment* spell.

Laws in some elven cities still carry a death sentence simply for possessing one of these amulets. The reasons behind those laws are forgotten to all but historians, but the risk of openly displaying such an amulet remains.

Arcanari

Wondrous item, rare

These twin books are always found together and are usually bound with heavy gold or silver covers. While not overtly magical, the detailed knowledge within them helps spellcasters of all types. Intensely studying both books, which takes at least one week per book, gives added insight into arcane magic and the art of casting spells. Individuals who take the time to perform such intensive study are rewarded by being able to add their proficiency bonus twice to Intelligence (Arcana) checks. This benefit can be gained only once.

Flute of the Black Sun

Wondrous item, uncommon (requires attunement)

Ancient elven runes adorn the black metal flute along with an elven symbol representing the sun. The alloy of silver, steel, and several rare minerals that create its black coloration helps prolong notes played on the flute and give it a beautiful tone. While playing the flute you gain advantage on Charisma (Performance) checks due to its exceptional craftsmanship. In addition, the flute can be used to cast *darkvision* once per day, and, if held or played, grants resistance to cold damage.

Iliachoam's Beasts and Saddles

Wondrous item, rare

Thick parchment pages are bound in a sturdy steel cover for preservation. This lengthy discussion of riding beasts and saddles provides many different hints and techniques for controlling animals while riding them. Unfortunately, the information doesn't mean much to anyone who doesn't already have some riding skill. Individuals who take the time to perform such intensive study are rewarded by being able to add their proficiency bonus twice to Wisdom (Animal Handling) checks that involve horses. This benefit can be gained only once.

Iliachoam's Trainer's Guide

Wondrous item, rare

Bound in dragon hide and magically preserved, this thick text gives detailed descriptions of various training methods for a wide variety of beasts. Descriptions of the various training techniques presumes a great deal of background knowledge; it is unlikely anyone other than a skilled animal trainer could garner much from this text. Individuals who take the time to perform such intensive study are rewarded by being able to add their proficiency bonus twice to Wisdom (Animal Handling) checks to train animals. This benefit can be gained only once.

INSTRUMENTS OF THE VEARLIK
Wondrous item, rare

This heavily detailed description of flutes and whistles made by a strange tribe of mountain orcs is interesting only to the most dedicated bard. The book describes the creation of various flutes and how each design creates a different timbre or pitch. Individuals who take the time to perform such intensive study are rewarded by being able to add their proficiency bonus twice to Charisma (Perform) checks. This benefit can be gained only once.

JAEREL'S JUNGLE GUIDE
Wondrous item, rare

This odd book is bound with, and written on, jungle leaves magically preserved and protected. The detailed descriptions of jungle plants and creatures within might be somewhat outdated, but the information is presented in a straightforward, albeit dry, manner. Individuals who take the time to perform such intensive study are rewarded by being able to add their proficiency bonus twice to Wisdom (Survival) checks made in jungles. This benefit can be gained only once.

RAINBOW BRACERS
Wondrous item, unique (requires attunement)

Swirls of color move slowly across the surface of these strange silver bracers. The bracers are imbued with enough magic that they glow faintly in the darkness. In addition to granting a +1 bonus to AC, you can cast *mage armor* once per day with a duration of 10 hours. Unlike the standard spell, the *mage armor* called forth is visible as a faint, translucent swirl of color surrounding the wearer's body.

RAINBOW CROSSBOW
Weapon, unique

The wooden stock of this light crossbow has been painted with boldly colored stripes that somehow extend to the steel portions of the crossbow. This crossbow functions like a light crossbow that fires bolts cloaked in colored light. Regardless of color, the bolts do an additional 3 (1d6) radiant damage to all forms of undead. Colored bolts do no additional damage to normal living creatures.

RAINBOW RING
Ring, unique (requires attunement)

This special ring is one of Londar Brightrain's special creations. At first glance, the twisted silver ring appears to be tarnished, but a closer inspection reveals that the strange rainbow hues are part of its natural color. While wearing the ring you instinctively realize that you can call into existence a *rainbow staff* as per the spell created by Londar. Summoning the staff requires only your will and is a free action, but once done three times can't be done again until you have completed a long rest. Once conjured, the staff lasts for 10 minutes before disappearing. Although you must be proficient with a staff, each attack with the staff is made with a +3 bonus to hit and damage, and causes additional damage based on the accompanying table.

RAINBOW RING RESULTS

1d8	Color	Result
1–2	Red	3d4 fire damage
3	Orange	2d8 acid damage
4	Yellow	Target slowed as per the *slow* spell for 2 rounds (DC 15 Wisdom saving throw negates)
5	Green	2d8 poison damage and target poisoned until the end of their next turn (DC 15 Constitution saving throw negates)
6	Blue	3d6 lightning damage
7	Indigo	Target gains the stunned condition until the end of their next turn (DC 15 Wisdom saving throw negates)
8	Violet	2d8 thunder damage

Note that you cannot determine what type of energy is expended on a particular blow, so creatures with immunities may be unaffected or even healed by some attacks.

SPELL WAND
Wand, varies (requires attunement by a spellcaster)

A spell wand allows you to cast a single spell without material components. While holding it, you can use an action to expend 1 charge to cast the spell associated with the wand. You must be able to speak the command and point the wand at the target. If the spell has a range of touch, then you must touch the target with the wand, although you still use the wand's spell attack bonus to attempt the touch. In general, the wand casts the spell with the lowest possible spell slot. The rarity, save DC, spell attack modifier, number of charges, and charge refresh per 24 hours are shown below, depending on the level of spell stored in the wand.

Spell Level	Rarity	Save DC	Attack Bonus	Charges	Charge Refresh
Cantrip	Common	13	+5	10	1d6 + 4
1st	Uncommon	13	+5	10	1d6 + 4
2nd	Uncommon	13	+5	7	1d6 + 1
3rd	Rare	15	+7	7	1d6 + 1
4th	Rare	15	+7	7	1d6 + 1
5th	Very Rare	17	+9	4	1d3 + 1
6th	Very Rare	17	+9	4	1d3 + 1
7th	Very Rare	18	+10	3	1d3
8th	Legendary	18	+10	3	1d3
9th	Legendary	19	+11	3	1d3

Special Items and Relics

The following items are hidden in Londar's Library or the Treasure Chamber of Horgrim's Temple. *Horgrim's Pyramid* and *The White Eye* are evil items that need to be hidden or destroyed before they can be abused by evil creatures.

Decaying Book

This ancient book is bound with worn leather and is so old that the markings on the spine and covers have been almost completely worn off. It is written in an arcane language so ancient that only an avid historian would have a chance of deciphering it with a successful DC 20 Intelligence (History) check. Pictures in the book show clear representations of *Horgrim's Pyramid*, *Korik's Ruby*, and *The White Eye*. If interpreted, the book describes how to activate the pyramid using *The White Eye* and *Korik's Ruby* to create an area of darkness with a one-mile radius that quenches all normal and magical daylight. Pages describing the pyramid's origins and the process used to create it are worn and torn to the point of being incomprehensible.

Horgrim's Pyramid

Wondrous item, artifact (requires attunement)

This strange gold and silver pyramid has several interlocking layers that can be turned around a central axis. Runes along the sides hint at great power, and the pyramid glows with a variety of different magics when studied with *detect magic*, but there is no hint as to what the pyramid actually does. Knowledge gathered from the *Decaying Book* allows one to open the pyramid by placing *The White Eye* in a depression at its base. Once opened, a large, multifaceted ruby must be placed in a precise location inside the pyramid. Once these actions are complete, the pyramid reveals its powers to the person holding it if they are evil or gives them a powerful shock if they are not.

Once activated, the pyramid gives any evil creature holding it the power to create a magical darkness with a radius of 2 miles. Within this area, all light spells and light sources are half as effective, and all sunlight and daylight damage effects against undead are nullified. It also grants the possessor the power to use *control undead* on up to 100 HD worth of undead within a 1000-foot radius. In addition to these powers, the wielder can use the following spells 1/day as a 20th-level spellcaster: *animate dead* and *contact outer plane*. Holding or using *The White Eye* at the same time as *Horgrim's Pyramid* doubles the range and power of these effects. Using the pyramid exacts a price: The first day of use results in the loss of body hair and makes the subject sensitive to sunlight (disadvantage on ability checks, savings throws, attack rolls in direct sunlight). Continued use ages the subject one day for every hour of use. There is no saving throw against these effects and no way to reverse the aging.

Good characters who attempt to activate the pyramid must succeed at a DC 18 Constitution saving throw or suffer 28 (8d6) necrotic damage (half damage on a successful save) at the start of their turn until they no longer possess the artifact. Neutral characters who try to activate the pyramid must make the same saving throw or suffer 14 (4d6) necrotic damage (half damage on a successful save) at the start of their turn until they no longer possess the artifact.

Korik's Ruby

This large ruby has hundreds of carefully cut facets that focus light shined through the gem into a tight dot several feet away. The ruby is not magical but happens to be the original ruby created for use in *Horgrim's Pyramid*. It was stolen from a popular merchant house in Bard's Gate.

The White Eye

Wondrous item, artifact (requires attunement by an evil humanoid)

A powerful and deadly relic on its own, *The White Eye* is required to open and activate *Horgrim's Pyramid*. Stored in a hidden temple for thousands of years, there is no exact record of all the powers this item possesses. Made of a strange white metal, it is oblong and the shape and size of a human eye. Glowing runes and strange symbols cover its surface as a mere hint of its evil power. Any good or neutral being within 5 feet of the stone senses its evil emanations without the aid of any magic.

The intelligent item (Intelligence 18, Wisdom 7, Charisma 19; Communication: telepathy; senses: hearing and darkvision out to 120 ft.; lawful evil) treats anything that is not evil with disdain, spite, and hatred. Its sole purpose is to destroy good and spread evil, and it considers the creatures that "wield" it simply to be tools to use. Any nonevil creature touching the eye suffers 28 (8d6) necrotic damage with no saving throw allowed.

The eye can be used only by an evil humanoid and has two levels of use. The first level of use is where it is simply held in one's hand. At this level of use, the eye grants you the ability to cast *animate dead*, *banishment*, *darkvision*, *detect evil and good*, or *hallow* at will. When used at this level, the eye attempts to influence you (a successful DC 15 Wisdom to ignore) and convince you to tear out your own eye and use it as a replacement. Anyone bold — or foolish — enough to do so unlocks all the eye's powers and receives the following additional benefits: permanent *darkvision* and *detect evil and good*, and the ability to cast the following spells: at will: *zone of truth*, *true seeing*, 2/day; *stoneskin*, 1/day; *haste*, *globe of invulnerability*, and a +4 bonus to initiative checks. Using the eye in this manner results in a constant battle for control, with the eye assuming complete control of the creature's body when it finally wins.

Appendix E: New Spells

Etch Stone
1st level transmutation

Casting Time: 1 action
Range: Touch
Components: V, S
Duration: One hour

You can magically inscribe messages or text in stone using an ordinary quill for one hour after casting this spell. Any type of message, design, or rune created with the quill is permanently inscribed in the stone for anyone to see. Combining additional spells with an *etch stone* spell allows the caster to inscribe hidden or magical messages on simple stone walls. Scrolls or spellbooks can be created in stone if someone were willing to take all the extra time and expense.

Rainbow Spear
4th-level conjuration

Casting Time: 1 action
Range: 25 ft.
Components: V, S
Duration: Concentration, up to 1 minute

You focus energy to create a spear of a specific color and effect that is thrown as a magic attack. The caster must choose what color to make the spear with each color having a different special effect. Spears must be used within 10 rounds of their creation and can be touched only by the caster. These spears are very useful against targets that have specific weaknesses known by the caster. A successful hit inflicts 1d6 piercing damage plus the following special effects:

At higher levels: When you cast this spell using a spell slot of 6th level or higher, you generate an additional spear for each slot level above 5th.

Color	Effect
Red	1d6 fire damage
Orange	1d6 acid damage
Yellow	Target is slowed as per the *slow* spell
Green	1d6 poison damage, and the target gains the poisoned condition until the end of its next turn
Blue	1d8 lightning damage
Indigo	Target gains the stunned condition until the end of its next round
Violet	1d8 thunder damage

Rainbow Staff
5th-level conjuration

Conjuration (creation)
Casting Time: 1 action
Range: Touch
Components: V, S
Duration: Concentration up to 1 minute

You conjure a shimmering rainbow-colored staff of energy. While the staff does not last long, it is an excellent melee weapon for the wizard unlucky enough to find themselves toe-to-toe with their foes. Although the caster must be proficient with a staff, each attack with the staff is made as a touch attack and does 1d6 bludgeoning damage along with damage based on the following table:

1d8	Color	Effect
1–2	Red	1d6 fire damage
3	Orange	1d6 acid damage
4	Yellow	Target is slowed as per the *slow* spell
5	Green	1d6 poison damage, and the target gains the poisoned condition until the end of its next turn.
6	Blue	1d8 lightning damage
7	Indigo	Target gains the stunned condition until the end of its next round
8	Violet	1d8 thunder damage.

Note that you cannot determine what type of energy is expended on a particular blow so creatures with immunities may be unaffected or even healed by some attacks.

Teleport Other
9th-level conjuration

Casting Time: 1 action
Range: 30 ft.
Components: V, S
Duration: Instant

You direct magical energies at any target size large or smaller within 30 feet to teleport the target to a specific location. The targets must succeed at a Wisdom saving throw or be teleported. The caster must be very familiar with the teleport destination. Any attempt to teleport a target into a solid object, underwater, or a location not firmly known to the caster results in automatic failure. While this spell can't be used to directly injure a target, it can certainly remove a specific victim from battle. Londar Brightrain created the spell to trap a wide variety of creatures for experiments performed in the caverns beneath his mansion.

NECROMANCER
Games™